CHANGING TIDES

Dutch Jones

DEDICATION

I am always appreciative of my family who allow me the time and support to write. I am always appreciative of my readers who motivate me to write more. Thank you for your ongoing support.

CONTENTS

ACKNOWLEDGMENTS

Thank you for taking another journey with me. I have great respect for all readers who are willing to become impassioned in a story. My job is to help you disconnect from this moment and take you to a different place. My wish for you is that you are always entertained by my stories; if you are, I have done my job.

THE STORM

The shoot for the television commercial was a great success. Everything the ad agency could hope for: the client was ecstatic. Everyone knew they had chosen the perfect person to launch the new beauty product line. That night at the wrap party, the only person who wasn't happy was the star of the commercial and certainly the center of attention: Jono. 'Supermodel' can't describe the amount of status, clout, exposure, or the size of the fees that is Jono. All this by age twenty-three. The party was a-raging, invited guests only to this high-level event. The house on the beach in Hawaii was filled to capacity. Actors, models, musicians, agents: everyone who was anyone who happened to be on the island that night was there.

Jono started drinking before she left her hotel for the party: she needed to get numb. Her boyfriend Troy was not happy. The arguing started the minute they stepped into the hotel room; it restarted the minute they stepped into the limousine. Jono wanted to be alone, she didn't want to talk, she didn't want to have another argument with Troy. She was tired, she wanted to sleep. Troy was not letting up, pushing Jono hard. He'd been in her face all day for no reason. Troy pushed to make his presence known, his ego needed to be in charge; it was important to him to think he could control Jono. He hated it when Jono got drunk, which lately was more often than not; it used to be fun, now it was embarrassing. Jono couldn't take it anymore and threw her drink in Troy's face. She demanded the limousine stop, and started to get out. Troy grabbed her arm to stop her. He forcibly pulled her back into the car; Jono screamed; she tried to hit Troy in the face, scratching at him like a trapped cat. Troy pulled the door shut and demanded the driver start driving.

As the car pulled up to the house, hundreds of people were waiting outside. It looked more like a movie opening than a party. Troy got out of the limousine first, then held out his hand to help Jono out of the car, cameras poised and ready. To everyone's surprise, especially Troy's, Jono got out of the limo on the other side of the car. Troy had no choice and played it off because of the cameras, but he was pissed.

"Jono is here, everyone!" he yelled as Jono came around the car. Everyone started to clap and call out her name, camera flashes lighting up the dark. Troy walked up to her and leaned in close. "Embarrass me like that again…" he threatened. Jono smiled as she tugged on the bottom of her short, tight dress to straighten it out. Just then her manager Maxwell approached her, interrupting anything else Troy was about to say.

"Are you okay?"

"I'm fine."

Maxwell gave Troy a dirty look; Troy wanted to strike out at him, but resisted. Maxwell smiled, then took Jono by the arm and escorted her to the front of the house where the cameras and media were waiting.

"Jono, what are you wearing?" one of the reporters yelled out while flashes from all the cameras were blinding her. *One of the stupidest questions I ever get asked*, she thought to herself. "It's not Troy Garrett!" she answered sharply with a big smile. Everyone laughed, except Troy. After the necessary amount of publicity photos had been taken, Maxwell again took Jono's arm and escorted her inside the house where the party was well underway. Troy had already gone in sometime earlier.

Within steps of the front door Jono was hit from all sides. Everyone wanted to say hi, congratulate her, or just be close enough to be in a photo with her. Jono was already starting to suffocate. Maxwell took charge as he always does and managed the well-wishers. "Okay, guys... Jono is here to celebrate, too! Let her get a drink and say hello to the host and I'm sure you will all have plenty of time to say hi in a bit... okay?" he politely asked the small crowd. The crowd dispersed: no one wanted to piss off Jono and potentially lose a chance to talk with her.

"Thanks, Max, I thought I was going to lose it!" Jono told him.

"I understand, but there are some people you have to say hi to," he reminded her.

"I know. Stay close, I want to get this over with as fast as possible," she commanded. Maxwell followed behind, all smiles, waving, shaking hands, doing his job.

The house was enormous. After entering through huge wood and glass double front doors you were standing in a small foyer. It had two marble columns at the steps which led down into the main part of the house. From the foyer Jono looked over the crowded room. More marble columns were wrapped around the room, giving it a circular feeling. There were two large fountains on either side of the room, one with a mermaid atop and the other with a shark. *A man's house for sure*, Jono smiled. The room had two bars, each with its own large saltwater aquarium behind them. The room had several sitting areas with many couches and chairs. But most important was the view! The ocean side of the house had no walls: open to the elements, the smells, the tropical breeze. The view. A magnificent view of the Pacific Ocean. Jono was spellbound.

Jono and Maxwell didn't get too deep into the party when they were approached by Josh, the head of the ad agency that hired Jono for the commercial. "Hi, guys! I'm so glad you could make it. We were starting to get a little worried," he confessed. Jono smiled and reached out her hand so Josh could shake it. Maxwell knew this was going to be a rough night.

"Jono is so happy to be here. I just need to get her a drink," Maxwell explained. Jono turned and looked at Maxwell with a smile only he would understand.

"Oh... of course. Right this way." Jono and Maxwell followed. On the way to the bar, Jono was stopped many times by people who wanted to say hi, take a picture with her, or hug her. Josh pushed himself to the front of the lines. "What would you like?" Josh asked Jono. Maxwell answered for her.

"Champagne would be great."

"Sure, of course." Josh requested three champagnes from the bartender.

"Thank you, Josh, that's very kind." Jono finally spoke up. Maxwell smiled in relief. Just as Josh was about to say something, Troy walked up. "I see you got your drink," he said rather smartly. "Yes," Jono answered.

"Can I talk to you for a minute... in private?" he requested.

"No, I'm sorry, Troy, Jono can't right now. There are several people Jono needs to visit with, and we just got here, so maybe later," Maxwell said sternly. Troy didn't like the answer; Jono didn't say anything or express anything. Disgruntled, Troy just walked away. "Fine."

Troy Garrett is the Hollywood epitome of a wannabe. Young, good-looking, athletic, high-energy with a major chip on his shoulder. He's tall, over six foot, with short, dark hair that he wears slicked back. *Tall, dark and handsome* is how he refers to himself. He came to Hollywood like so many before him looking to claim his fame. Problem is, he can't act, hence the chip. To date he has been in two movies, no speaking parts, and in one of them his part never made it off the cutting-room floor. He has had some success as a male model, which is how he and Jono met. About a year ago, Jono was on a shoot in Brazil for a very high-end bathing suit company; Troy was there as background with several other guys. One night after a beach party, Jono and Troy got together and had been together ever since. Troy had not had an acting or modeling job since. He traveled with Jono, lived with her, and basically lived off of her.

In the beginning it was good: Jono liked Troy. She wasn't bothered by the fact that he didn't work, she liked the company and having a male hunk on her arm was good for pictures. To appease Troy's need for attention, every now and then Jono would get him some modeling work: all she had to do was ask. But it was important that Troy thought he got the work on his own, a secret only Jono and Maxwell knew. It was his overpowering personality and self-confidence (some would say ego) that first attracted Jono to him. That wore off quickly. But Troy was relentless, he was the king of car salesmen, never giving up. He and Jono would have fights, some epic, always making the news. They'd break up, sometimes it would last a few days, but ultimately Troy's persistence would win out and they would get back together. Troy's control over Jono was strong: Jono hated it, Maxwell hated it. Maxwell had nothing but disdain for Troy since the first minute he met him. Troy was a delicate subject with Jono: every time he would voice his opinion, or try to, she would shut him out, sometimes for days.

Jono knew that Troy was not good for her, she knew he was not a good person. He had this power over her that she hated and loved at the same time. Maybe it was her upbringing: Jono's mom worked hard to put Jono down whenever she could. She would tell Jono, even as a very young child, that she wasn't good enough. One time Jono won a trophy at school for being the best reader in her fifth-grade class. Excited to tell her mother about it, as any kid would, she ran home to show her. When she entered the house she called out to her mom. Her mom came walking out from the kitchen with a glass of bourbon in her hand, her normal lunchtime meal.

"What the hell are you yelling about?!"

"Look, Mom!" Jono proudly held up her trophy with a big smile on her face. She was gleaming with excitement.

"Best reader." Her mom read the plate on the trophy with no emotion. "Best reader. What exactly does that mean?"

"I'm the best reader in my class, Mom!" She stood, struggling to keep the trophy over her head with her neck stretched out straining to look up at her mom.

"Well, that's just stupid. What the hell good is this? It's not like this trophy is going to get you a job!" She raised her voice, then snatched the trophy out of Jono's hands and threw it across the room where it crashed into the wall, breaking the top off. Jono turned and looked at her trophy sitting on the floor, broken. She hesitated; her mom stood there with a smirk of confidence on her face. Jono screamed and ran to her room.

"Don't think I'm cleaning that up!" her mother yelled after her.

"It is a great pleasure to have you in my home," her host Dan Visage told her as he finished his kiss on the right cheek, then the left cheek. Dan was one of the largest movie producers in the business; he had been for some time and this house was one of many examples of his success.

"Thank you, Mr. Visage, I'm honored," Jono responded sincerely.

"Oh please: Dan. Please call me Dan."

"Thank you, Dan. This is such a beautiful home, I can't imagine what it must be like living here."

"I wish I lived here!" he joked. "Unfortunately I only get out here once or twice a year. Sadly this beautiful house mostly sits empty. By the way, any time you want to use it, you just give me a call, it's yours, staff and all." He smiled. Maxwell immediately got excited.

"That's very generous of you... Dan. Thank you. You never know I might just take you up on that." Jono smiled back. Maxwell got more excited.

"Great. By the way, have you seen out back yet?" Dan asked Jono and the group standing around them.

"No I'm sorry, I haven't had the chance, but I'd love to."

"Well, let me be your tour guide then." He took Jono by the arm, and they and about twenty other people proceeded outside to the large, two-level back deck.

"This is just magnificent!" Jono exclaimed about the view.

"This is truly amazing!" Maxwell added.

"I'm so glad you like it. The most peaceful place in the world," Dan told them. "Clears my head."

"I can see why." Jono smiled. Dan was right, Jono already felt better: between the light tropical breeze, the sound of the waves, the palm trees whisking about, the smell of the salt, and the strong aroma of the flowers, she felt like she was being transported somewhere else. She closed her eyes and took in a deep breath.

"Good, right?" Dan asked.

"No. Great." Jono held out her arms, feeling the breeze run over them. "Amazing."

"Jono, I hate to break this up, but we really need to meet with the clients," Maxwell reminded her.

"Yes. Of course we do," she responded in a business-like tone. "Thank you, Dan. Fantastic." Dan nodded.

Jono and Maxwell worked the party, making sure all those who needed to be seen with Jono were, and all those whom Jono needed to meet for career advancement and exposure she did. Maxwell had been pushing Jono for some time to get more into television or film. While Jono and Maxwell were fully engaged with a well-known television producer, Troy approached. "Love your work," he told the producer, a lame, typical, out-of-touch response when someone on the outside doesn't know who they're talking to who's on the inside. The man nodded. Troy turned his attention to Jono. "Can I talk to you?" Troy said to her, rather forcefully. Jono looked at Maxwell: he reluctantly nodded. "Excuse me," Jono told the producer. "No problem." Maxwell stayed behind, continuing the conversation.

Troy pulled Jono into a bedroom and closed the door behind them. "What's wrong with you?" he snapped at Jono.

"Me? What the hell is wrong with you? You do realize I'm working here?" she snapped back. "Or did you completely forget the concept of work?" Troy, without thinking, slapped Jono across the face with the back of his hand, hard, nearly knocking Jono down. Jono turned away; she wanted to cry but didn't. She wanted to scream but didn't. Jono's face was her money, she was pissed. She turned back to face Troy, holding her cheek. "How dare you!" she said, gritting her teeth.

"Jono, I'm so sorry, I didn't mean to, it just happened," he pleaded.

"Yeah, and this will be the last time this just happens!" She started to walk out the door.

"Jono, wait!" Troy yelled out, forcibly grabbing her arm. Without a second's hesitation, Jono whipped around and punched Troy in the face: this time she screamed out in pain. Troy took a good shot right to the eye. "That's going to bruise!" Jono told him, trying to shake off the pain in her hand. She turned and walked out of the room.

Covering her face with her hand, Jono walked right to Maxwell who was still talking to the same television producer. He acknowledged her as she approached, then he saw the redness on her face. "Will you excuse us?" Maxwell asked. "Of course. We'll talk later," the producer told him. Maxwell took Jono's arm and headed for the closest bathroom, trying to help cover her as he did. When they got into the bathroom, Maxwell closed and locked the door. Maxwell reached up and slowly pulled Jono's hand away from her face. Maxwell literally gasped. "Jono, what the hell happened?" Jono started to cry. Maxwell held her close to comfort her. "Honey, are you okay? This was Troy, wasn't it?" he said in a soft but stern voice. Jono simply nodded yes while her head still rested on Maxwell's chest.

"This has got to stop and it's going to stop now!" Maxwell said, a little too loudly. Jono pulled back.

"It's over. This time for real, I promise." Maxwell was not satisfied. "I need to find him," he told her, turning for the door.

"Maxwell, no! It's okay, he's already gone. I took care of it." Jono's cheek was red and swollen: she had a small scratch at the top of her cheek, likely from one of Troy's rings. Maxwell wet a hand towel with cold water and held it on Jono's face. Jono grimaced in pain. "That asshole... seriously."

"It's going to leave a nasty mark," he told her. Thankfully she didn't have any work for several weeks.

Jono and Maxwell stayed in the bathroom for quite some time until they were interrupted by their host, Dan. "Hey! Is everything okay in there?" he joked. "Yes, yes," Maxwell answered. "Just a little accident. We'll be right out."

"Oh, is there anything I can do?" Dan asked in a concerned voice.

"A little ice would be great," Maxwell answered back.

"Sure, no problem." Dan signaled one of his staff to go get the ice. The bathroom door slowly opened. First Maxwell came out, then Jono emerged holding the wet towel on her face.

"Oh my God, Jono, what happened?" Dan asked, visibly upset and very concerned.

"I'm fine," she smiled. "Stupid blonde thing, I wasn't paying attention and I walked face first into a corner." She tried to laugh it off. The staff person came back with a small bucket of ice. Maxwell took several pieces and put them into the hand towel. "Here, honey, this will help."

"Jono, I feel so bad. Is there anything I can do?" Dan asked her.

"Yes. A tall stiff drink would be great!" she joked but meant it.

Maxwell wanted to leave the party right away, but now Jono didn't want to go. She insisted they stay and finish what they came for. Several drinks later Jono was feeling no pain - if anything, she was feeling relieved. "I don't want to go back to my room at the hotel," she told Maxwell. "Of course. I wouldn't let you anyway. Tonight you're staying with me where I can keep an eye on you." Maxwell smiled at her. She reached up and gave him a little kiss on the cheek, "Ouch!" she yelped. "Oh honey." Jono laughed. "Funny," he said sarcastically, but still laughed with her.

The party was raging, in full force, even though it was well after 1:00 in the morning. Jono and Maxwell somehow got separated as they were moving about from person to person at the party. Jono's cheek was swollen and starting to show signs of bruising, but she wasn't feeling the pain anymore. Jono was way past her normal drunk levels and was on a tear. She stopped using the wall as the excuse for her face and was openly blaming her boyfriend, sort of joking about it; most laughed with her, not sure what to believe. The incident definitely made its way through the entire party. Many of the party guests wanted to take a photo with Jono with her face all red and bruised. Jono was so drunk she didn't care, and Maxwell was nowhere around to stop her.

After another hour or so Jono was spent: her face really started to hurt no matter how much she medicated, and she was ready to leave. She looked all over for Maxwell but couldn't find him anywhere. Every time she asked someone they quickly changed the subject to talk about her or ask her for something. It was all starting to crash down on her fast. She felt like she was going to get sick, so she headed for the bathroom: occupied. She looked around to see if she could find another one; she did and quickly headed toward it. As she did, the bathroom door opened: it was Troy. "Shit!" she said to herself. Troy didn't see her.

Jono turned and headed in the opposite direction as quickly as her wobbly legs could take her. She moved through the party, not stopping to talk with anyone. She walked out back onto the deck where several guests were hanging out talking and drinking. She darted down the side steps to the beach and ran toward the water, her shoes flipping off as she did. Not a minute too late, Jono crashed into the sand and started violently throwing up. She looked back at the house:

no one could hear her over the loud music, she was relieved. After getting sick a few more times she got up and moved closer to the water. She sat down, folded her knees and stared at the ocean, listening and watching. It was so peaceful.

SCUBA-DIVING LESSON

Jono sat there, thinking, sobbing, not sure of anything anymore. So successful, so many people in her life, yet she was lonely and sad. She continued to sob with her head down, resting on her arms. Suddenly she stopped crying, looked up at the ocean, then back at the party. Only one small group of people were out on the deck. Jono stood up and walked into the water, only far enough for the water to rush over her feet. The water was cool, it felt so good. The sound of the crashing waves was intoxicating. She turned and looked at the house again. No one was there anymore, they must have all gone inside. The floodlights from the house were only able to shine about halfway to the water. Jono didn't hesitate. She reached down and grabbed the bottom of her dress and proceeded to pull it up over her head. She turned and threw her dress up on the beach. With only a G-string on, she started slowly making her way deeper into the water. The waves were large, but she didn't care.

At first she handled the waves pretty well as they crashed close to shore. By the time she was waist-deep she was no longer in control: the waves were too big and too powerful. She was being pulled out to sea but she was too drunk to tell; even if she could, at this moment she didn't care. She could no longer touch the bottom, she had to start swimming to stay above the water. She was laughing and giggling, talking to herself. Then, like a silent attacker, Jono was hit from behind by a large wave, forcing her under the water. Jono was tossed and turned in every direction: it would have been easier to swim in a washing machine. She felt the ocean bottom and kicked as hard as she could to get to the surface. She gasped for air. A second later she was hit by another powerful wave, and once again she was at the waves' mercy, trying desperately to hold her breath. She made her way to the surface only long enough to suck in some air and scream for help. Bam! Another wave pounded her body, forcing her back to the ocean floor. She was losing strength, she was losing her willpower. She nearly blacked out, but she made it to the surface one last time: she tried to yell but almost nothing came out. She could see the lights from the house: she tried to wave, but her arms felt like lead. In seconds she gave into the waves and slowly started to sink to the bottom.

Jono was done, she was gone, succumbed to the power of the ocean. Her body collapsed on the sandy bottom. Jono's body rolled around with the tide, her long, beautiful hair flowing all around her. Out of nowhere a hand stretched out to grab her. The man got a hold of one of her arms and pulled. He pushed off hard and rocketed them both to the surface. He gasped for air. Jono was limp, no life. The man struggled hard against the large and powerful waves to get Jono out of the water; he knew every second counted, it might already be too late. He finally got her to the white water where he was able to pick her up and carry her the rest of the way out of the water. The man set her gently down on the beach well away from the breaking waves. He kneeled down in the sand right next to her. Jono was lifeless, her lips were blue, and her face was pale. The man carefully moved her hair off her face. He leaned over and put his ear right on Jono's lips: no breathing. He put his ear on her bare chest: a heartbeat! The man acted as if he knew exactly what he was doing. First he turned Jono on her side and forcibly hit her on her back with the palm of his hand: she coughed up some water but was still not breathing. He rolled her on her back again, then moved up to her head and cocked it back with his hands. He opened her mouth, reached in and pushed her tongue to one side. He pinched Jono's nose with one hand while holding her neck with the other, leaned over, and put his mouth all the way over Jono's. He blew three hard blows into her, watching her chest inflate. No reaction. He listened again for a heartbeat: it was faint but it was there. He repositioned himself to get a better grip on her neck, pulled her head back, and blew again three times, even harder. He looked and listened for anything. No reaction. The man was getting desperate: he rolled Jono back on her side, pointing her face toward the sand. He struck her several more times on her back with as much force as was safe. There was a loud, scary sound that came out of her, then a gurgling sound, and suddenly Jono threw up, water spraying out of her lungs like a fire hose. Jono's body fought hard to breathe, to survive. She shook uncontrollably for over a minute. The man waited until Jono stopped and her body calmed down. He rolled her on her back, took off his shirt and elevated her head. Jono was breathing on her own.

The man was leaning in close to Jono, staring at her face. He was surprised at how helpless she looked. Color was slowly coming back. Then he heard something and turned toward the house. "Jono!" Troy screamed, running as fast as he could toward the man. Several other party guests were right behind. Maxwell couldn't yell, he was using all the energy he had to run. Troy didn't slow down: he tackled the man so hard it knocked them both into the water. First the man stood. He started to say something when he was struck hard in the face by Troy. The man collapsed, knocked out cold.

Maxwell got to Jono first. "Oh my God, Jono! What did you do?" He sat and put her head in his lap. He stroked her hair. "Call an ambulance!" he screamed. "Already on the way!" Dan said as he ran up.

"Is she okay?"

"I'm not sure. She's breathing, though." Troy dragged the man out of the water and dropped him on the beach. "How is she?" he asked.

"She's out, I'm not sure," Maxwell said, tearing up. "Who is that guy?" he asked.

"Not sure, some beach bum, I think. I think he was attacking Jono, so I knocked him out."

"I know that guy," Dan spoke up. "Well, I don't really know him, but I see him once in a while around town or down here on the beach. My staff call the cops on him all the time for trespassing," he added.

Maxwell looked up at Troy, "Well, maybe it was a good thing he was trespassing today," Troy smirked. "We don't know what he did or didn't do: why do you always have to be such an ass?" Troy stated. He moved closer to Jono and picked up her hand. "It's going to be okay, baby... everything will be alright. I'm here with you." Maxwell felt like he was going to be sick. He was so done with Troy he wanted to lash out, but right now Jono needed to be his only concern. *I'll deal with this prick later*, he thought. Moments later you could hear sirens coming from the emergency vehicles as they got closer. Jono was rushed to the hospital, and the man who saved her life was taken to jail.

Maxwell stayed with Jono all night in her hospital room, in ICU. The doctors explained to Maxwell that Jono hadn't been attacked in any way, that actually she nearly drowned. They were able to determine that her lungs were full of salt water, and she was only seconds away from being a statistic. "Whoever it was who pulled her out of the water saved her life. And trust me, they knew what they were doing," the doctor explained to Maxwell.

Troy tried several times to get into Jono's room, but because she was in ICU and he wasn't related, Maxwell was able to keep him out. Everyone knew who Maxwell was, so he was an exception. Troy tried calling Maxwell so many times he finally turned off his phone.

Between Troy and all the reporters his phone was in a constant state of buzzing.

Nearly a day had gone by. Maxwell only left Jono's side to get something to eat or to go to the bathroom; the only people he would contact were Jono's other staff: he kept them in the loop as much as possible. There were too many reporters, paparazzi and news vans camped in front of the hospital to count. Maxwell dreaded it, but knew at some point he'd have to make a statement with the doctors. He was going to wait as long as possible. Flowers were pouring in by the hundreds, to the point where the hospital didn't know what to do. "Leave this one, and distribute all the rest to as many rooms as you can," Maxwell instructed. "Please start with the children's ward," he requested. "I know that's what Jono would want." The hospital staff did just that. Late that night, Jono made some mumbling sounds, like maybe she was having a dream or a nightmare. Maxwell raced to her side, but she didn't wake up.

Maxwell was in a deep sleep in the uncomfortable hospital chair when he was awoken. "Max?" a meek voice asked. Maxwell jumped to his feet and wiped his eyes. "Oh thank God, you're awake." He went to her, leaned over her bed, and gave her a long hug. He was softly sobbing with his head buried in her neck. Jono smiled, then gently nudged him up. "What happened?" she asked her manager and friend. Maxwell, exhausted both physically and emotionally, laughed. "Where would you like me to start?" He sat down next to her on the bed. "You gave me a scare that I never want to go through again," he softly scolded. "I nearly lost you." His eyes started to well up again.

Maxwell told Jono the whole story, leaving out no details. Jono could barely remember anything about the party, let alone the near drowning. She didn't even remember going into the water. As Maxwell told the story, Jono listened intently. About the only thing she actually remembered was being struck by Troy. "Where is that goon?" she asked, getting more strength in her voice. "I'm not sure," Maxwell told her. "Listen, Max, I don't want to see him. I don't want to see him ever again! Okay?" she told him as she was getting visibly upset. "Relax, Jono, I'll take care of it." Maxwell smiled.

Early the next morning Maxwell walked into the police station and went to the front desk. "Can I help you?" the officer asked.

"Yes, is that guy from the Jono incident still here?" Maxwell asked the officer.

"Yes, he is. Mr. Mike Johnson is scheduled to be arraigned later today."

"Arraigned? For what?" Maxwell asked rather sharply.

"Assault."

"Assault?" Maxwell was a little taken aback. "Why? Who filed assault charges?"

The officer got on his computer and looked it up.

"It appears it was a guy named Troy Garrett, he filed the charges," the police officer told him. It took everything Maxwell had not to explode right there. "I see. Well, can you tell me how much his bail is?"

"No not yet, not until he's been arraigned. I'll know after that. Why?"

"Because, he did not assault anyone... In fact, he's a hero. He saved Jono, you know Jono? He saved her life!" Maxwell was getting really upset.

"No, I didn't know that. But it doesn't matter anyway, he'll still have to go before the judge. It's out of my hands," the officer explained.

"Fine. What time is the arraignment?"

"Two. At the county courthouse."

"Thank you."

Maxwell went straight to the hotel and straight to Jono's room. He bolted through the door to find Troy sitting in a robe eating a large breakfast. "What are you doing?" Maxwell asked. "I'm eating breakfast. Why? What does it look like I'm doing?" He smirked and took another bite. "Why did you file assault charges against the man who saved Jono's life?" Troy put his fork down and wiped his face with a linen napkin.

"Because he assaulted me, that's why."

"What?! Are you completely mental?" Maxwell wasn't holding back. Troy stood up and threw his napkin down on the table. Maxwell may have been slightly taller but Troy was a lot younger and certainly much stronger. Maxwell stepped forward. "What, are you going to beat me up, too?" he asked sarcastically. "That would be preferred, then I can file assault charges against you!" Maxwell yelled at Troy. Troy sat back down. "I was only messing with you," Troy explained. "Yea." Maxwell secretly gulped.

"Here's what you need to know," Maxwell started. "What do you think Jono's reaction will be when she finds out you filed assault charges against the man who saved her life? Did you think about that? Dummy?"

"What did you call me?" Troy stood back up.

"If you ever, and I mean ever, think you have a prayer of seeing Jono again, I highly suggest you be at the courthouse today at 2:00 and drop the charges against this man. Otherwise, not only will you have to deal with the wrath of Jono, but I'm pretty sure there will be about six or seven eyewitnesses that will come forward and say you're the one who assaulted Mr. Johnson." Maxwell smiled. Troy sat there, continuing to eat his breakfast. He tried to act like he wasn't phased.

"And if you do... I have a little gift for you." Maxwell walked over to the table and dropped an envelope on it.

"What's this?"

"A ticket back to LA for later this afternoon," Maxwell explained. Troy threw the envelope on the floor.

"You're nuts! I'm not going anywhere. Jono needs me and I'm staying right here."

"Yes. I figured you'd day that. That's why you need to open the envelope." Maxwell spoke confidently. Troy stared Maxwell down. He reached down to the floor and picked up the envelope. He pulled out the airline ticket, then a business card. The card was that of a Peter

Trexler, a well-known film producer and director. On the back of the card was written, Eight am, Beverly Hills Hotel.

"What's this?"

"It's your ticket."

"I can see it's my ticket, what's with the card?"

"Like I said, it's your ticket." Maxwell was pushing Troy pretty hard. He could see he was getting pissed, which Maxwell was fully enjoying. "Mr. Trexler wants you in his next film, it starts shooting tomorrow. If you're not there, no job. Like I said, it's your ticket." Maxwell smiled with a certain amount of satisfaction.

"Is this for real?"

"Call him if you'd like, but I don't think I would."

"Why not? That's a good idea. Then I'll know if you're just playing me or not."

"Fine. But Mr. Trexler is a very busy man who is about to start shooting a tremendously expensive film. I'm sure he'd love to hear from one of his lower-level, non-established actors."

"Fine!"

"I love my job," Maxwell said quietly as he left the suite.

VACATION WITH
CONSEQUENCES

M ike walked out of the county courthouse a free man. Sore
but free. He had a couple of bruised ribs and his face was
pretty banged up, but no broken bones. He stepped into the sun and
smiled. *That's what I get*, he thought to himself. He turned and started
walking down the sidewalk in the direction of the beach. Troy *is* a
beach bum, Dan was right. But in his case he chooses to be. He left
the world and everything in it behind. He has given up, on himself,
on people and sometimes on life.

Two and a half years ago, Mike's life could not have been much
better. He was a strong, athletic, tall, twenty-seven-year-old man. He
was big in stature and big in life, outgoing and friendly with everyone. He was a fireman in Denver, Colorado, where he lived with his
wife of five years and their three-year-old daughter Macie. At twenty-
seven, Mike receive an unexpected but well-deserved promotion: he
was made captain of his station. No one who worked with him was
surprised at the promotion, he earned it. As a result, Mike and his

young family decided to celebrate by taking their first real family vacation. Mike wanted to go to Hawaii, a place he had been many times. His wife Jessie really wanted to go to South Carolina where most of her family was, but she knew how much Mike wanted to take her to Hawaii, so she agreed. Mike was excited: this would be Jessie's first trip to Hawaii, and he knew after she had experienced it she would love it as much as he did.

Mike grew up in Southern California five miles from the beach. Starting at about nine, every spare moment in his life he was in the water surfing, sometimes with friends, but often alone. By the time he was in his late-teens he got really good and even won a couple of local competitions. Mike was one of those guys who, from an early age, always knew what he wanted to do when he grew up: he was going to be a fireman. He took the fireman's test while still in college and graduated from the academy a week after turning twenty-one. He was hoping to get work in California, especially anywhere near the beach, but no one was hiring at that time. It didn't take long when the Denver Fire Department hired him. Mike had never been to Colorado before: it was a long way from the beach. Mike loved Colorado instantly. Everything about it was who he was, he just didn't know it. He quickly became an excellent skier, and in the summer water-skiing was a regular thing. Although he missed surfing and the ocean, Mike loved being in the mountains of Colorado.

During Mike's second winter, on one of his days off, he was on the slopes skiing with a buddy. As he was ripping down the main slope for his last run of the day, he saw a woman skiing in front of him who was cut off by a young skier, sending her into a barrel roll at high speed, skis and snow flying everywhere. By the time she came to a stop, her right leg was broken. Mike quickly skied over to her. He didn't have to look at the leg to know it was broken. He rolled the women on her back, then jammed his ski poles into the snow below her to keep her from sliding down the mountain. He wiped some of the snow and hair from her face. The young woman lay there: she had to be in a great deal of pain, but was smiling. Mike was puzzled and it showed on his face. He smiled back. "Are you okay?" He continued to wipe off the rest of the snow, looking for any other signs of injury. "I always wanted to be rescued by a young handsome man," she said softly. Mike laughed, but that was all it took.

Mike spent the winter nursing his girlfriend back to health, although she didn't really need it. Jessie was a world-class athlete, a top-level skier, no stranger to broken bones or dealing with pain. Jessie and Mike didn't just love each other, they weren't just friends or skiing buddies, they were a team. One year later, on the exact date they met, they were married, at the bottom of the slope where they first met. It was a magnificent spectacle with all the fire trucks and police cars flashing their lights and blasting their sirens, but then it was Mike and Jessie: nothing less for the favored couple.

Mike and Jessie were so looking forward to the vacation: a much-needed break for both of them. A chance to get away from the snow and spend some quality family time, just relaxing. Even though Macie was only three, she was already proving she was going to be an athlete. Before she turned one she could swim; by age two she was skiing (with help from Mom or Dad) down some bunny hills. She was a talker and a walker: both she did very fast. Her parents loved it. One could easily spend twenty minutes having a conversation with Macie, fully animated with hands, feet and head. Only knowing a few actual words never slowed her down.

The day they landed in Honolulu it was raining, but it didn't matter: Mike was right. The minute Jessie stepped out of the airport she was in awe. She drew in a deep smell, absorbing the aroma that is only Hawaii. She got it, and they hadn't even left the airport yet. Mike was super-excited. After they checked into the hotel it was straight to the beach. "Wow." Jessie smiled while squishing her toes into the white sand. Macie was in a full sprint to the water, with her dad right behind her. It was a great day, a special day, a perfect day.

Mike was unraveling, he was so excited to show his wife his surfing skills. It had been nearly six years since Mike has stepped foot in the ocean. He proved in his first couple of attempts that surfing is not like riding a bike: he had some pretty bad wipe-outs. He was starting to scare his wife, but on the third attempt he was back on his bike, riding the wave like he always had. *He is really good*, she thought; Jessie was truly impressed. Mike took Macie out on his board several times to play around in the shallow water on the tiny waves, and she screamed with excitement. Jessie tried her hand at surfing, but in the end thought she would be better serving as the family cheerleader.

The week-long vacation was flying by. Every day was spent at the beach, swimming, surfing and building sandcastles. Jessie was not ready to go home: she had got the bug in a big way. On the last night, Mike wanted to do something special. They already did a luau, learned to do the hula and a host of other touristy things. Mike chartered a small sailboat that would take them on a sunset cruise. The boat pulled out of the harbor; Macie was losing her mind she was having so much fun. They all got to help hoist the mainsail: it was a new experience for all of them. While Macie was busy explaining to the captain what he needed to do and which direction they needed to go, Mike and Jessie sat back with their Mai Tai cocktails and tried to take it all in. "This is unbelievable," Jessie told Mike.

"I'm so glad you like it here. That means a lot to me," he told her.

"I know. Honestly," she smiled. "I'm already thinking about when we can come back." Mike chuckled. Suddenly, out of nowhere, a huge powerboat crashed full speed into the back of the sailboat. No one saw it coming, no one heard it coming. The powerboat ripped through the sailboat like a saw through wood, nearly cutting the boat in half. There was no time to react. Mike flew off the side of the sailboat, landing in the water, hurt but able to swim. The sailboat was quickly sinking. "JESSIE!" Mike screamed. He was spinning all around the water trying to see where she or Macie might be, but he saw no one. With a broken leg he struggled to swim over to the boat. "JESSIE!"

he screamed again. The sailboat was now fully engulfed by the sea: it sank in seconds. Mike tried to swim down with it, but it was sinking too fast and the water was way too deep. He resurfaced. "MACIE!" he screamed as loud as he could. Then he saw someone in the water about twenty yards away. He swam as fast as he could. Other boats in the area started to pull up: several people jumped into the water to try to help Mike. "My wife and my daughter! I can't find them!" He got to the person he saw floating in the water: it was Jessie. She was floating on her stomach, her neck was broken.

"Mike knew there was nothing he could do but he tried anyway. "No! No! This can't be! Oh my God, Jessie, please don't leave me." Mike got quiet and talked right into Jessie's ear. "I can't be without you. I need you, please don't leave me." He kissed her on her lips. "Hey, mister!" someone yelled out. Mike snapped out of it. "Macie!" he yelled. "Is it my baby?" he screamed as he swam toward the guy who called out. "Is it my daughter, is she alright?" Mike yelled. As he got up to the boat several people were lifting Macie out of the water and onto the deck. "Is she alright?" he yelled as he got next to the boat. Two guys lifted Mike on-board, and he screamed in pain. Once on deck he crawled to Macie: her body was lifeless. Mike screamed at the people standing over her. "Get away, that's my daughter! I'm a fireman, help me!" he demanded. One big guy dragged Mike over to Macie. He quickly assessed her condition. She wasn't breathing and he couldn't feel a pulse. He got up on his one good knee. "Does anyone know CPR?" he called out. Nearly everyone said yes. "Okay you," he pointed to a young woman. "Please help me. You take the head and I'll do contractions." "Okay."

For fifteen minutes all the way back to the marina Mike and the young woman didn't stop. No one on-board said a word. One woman was praying out loud. Mike kept talking to Macie. "Come on, baby, you can do it. Come back to Daddy. Please, honey, I need you to breathe now," he would beg her. As the boat pulled into the marina, several fire trucks, police cars and two harbor patrol boats were waiting.

EMTs jumped on-board. One of them kneeled down opposite Mike. "Let me take over for a while," he said gently. Mike didn't look up or acknowledge his presence. "You're exhausted, let me help," the EMT insisted. Mike looked up at the EMT, a young Hawaiian man. Tears were streaming down Mike's face. "It's okay, I've got this," the EMT told him.

Within minutes Macie was in an ambulance on her way to the hospital. Mike wanted to go with her, but the police and the firemen restrained him so they could check him out. He fought and yelled, but it wasn't going to do any good. He tried to stand, but as soon as he put pressure on his broken leg he passed out.

The next morning Mike woke up in the hospital, his leg cast from his foot to his groin. He lifted his head to look around. In his room there was a doctor, a nurse, two police officers and a priest. "Macie?" Mike asked, looking at the priest. The priest lowered his head. Mike began screaming so loud he had to be sedated. He awoke several hours later, sobbing. Before he had even opened his eyes, the reality was consuming him. He felt someone pick up his hand. Mike opened his eyes: it was a nurse. "Mr. Johnson, is there anything I can do for you, anything I can get you?" she asked sincerely. Mike turned his head away from her and started to cry. He'd never felt this kind of pain; he started to get nauseous. Someone picked up his other hand. Mike opened his eyes again: it was the priest. "I'm here. If you need anything, just ask," the priest told him. Mike nodded. "Where's my wife and daughter?" he asked the priest. A natural reaction.

"I'm so sorry, Mike, they're no longer with us. They are at peace with God." The priest squeezed Mike's hand. Mike bit his lip hard; he knew, but he was hoping somehow it was all a bad dream. "Can I see them?" he asked the priest. "No, I'm afraid not. That's just not possible," he tried to explain. Mike knew why. He started to cry again, but there were no more tears left. A policeman stepped up from behind the priest. "Mr. Johnson, I'm sorry, I know this is a terrible time for you, I am truly sorry for your loss… but would it be possible for me to ask you a few questions? I need to get your statement for our report. We have someone in custody and we need to clarify a few things," he explained.

"Custody?"

"Yes, the driver of the other boat. He's been arrested for murder."

"Murder?" Mike questioned with a surprised look on his face.

"Yes, sir... He, the driver of the other boat, was so intoxicated he passed out at the wheel, full throttle. He never saw the sailboat and never felt the impact. His boat only stopped because it ran out of fuel twenty minutes later," the officer explained. Mike nodded. "Okay."

Mike didn't remember much, and what he did remember he wished he hadn't. With a nurse on one side and the priest on the other, the police officer explained what happened, or what they had pieced together at that point. Mike learned that the driver of the powerboat was also the owner. A young man, twenty-two, from Saudi Arabia. He and his friends had been partying on the beach all day, then they decided to take the boat out. Three guys, drunk and still drinking. By the time the boat hit the breakwater, the driver, who was at full speed, passed out. The other two guys jumped out of the boat almost immediately, amazingly unharmed. The policeman told Mike that, had they not been so drunk, they would have surely sustained multiple injuries if not killed themselves.

From that point the police officer could only surmise what happened, but it didn't take a veteran detective to put it together. The powerboat at full speed, out of control, slammed into the back of the sailboat, and all but the captain were thrown into the water. The captain was killed instantly. Jessie sustained a broken neck and several other injuries that the policeman would not elaborate on. She was also killed instantly. Macie was thrown for some distance and was knocked out when she hit the water. She drowned; her other injuries were only minor.

Hearing all this left Mike emotionless. He turned away from the police officer and buried his head in his pillow. Everyone left his room. Every night for three nights Mike had to be heavily sedated, not as much to deal with the pain in his leg, but more for the pain in his heart. His own fire chief and friends from Denver tried to call many times, but Mike would take no calls. His chief even had the local fire department captain stop in to check on Mike, but Mike refused all visitors. One afternoon the priest came into Mike's room. He closed the door and pulled a chair up next to Mike's bed. Mike looked at him, but said nothing.

"Mike, I have to talk to you about something. It's important and we can't wait any longer." Mike nodded. "We have to make arrangements for your wife and daughter, I need to know what you want to do," he explained. Unfortunately Mike had already given this a great deal of thought. He sat up further in his bed and adjusted the pillow under his broken leg. "I'm assuming you want to take them home, to be with family and friends," the priest said. Mike didn't answer. "The doctors say you should be well enough to travel in a day or two, so you can travel with them." The mere thought of flying with his family in boxes underneath him, mixed in with the rest of the luggage, made him angry. "I can make all the flight arrangements for you, you just need to let me know when you..." "No!" Mike blurted out, interrupting the priest. "Oh. I'm sorry. I'm just trying to help," the priest explained.

"It's not that, Father... Honestly I appreciate what you're doing, I appreciate all the things you've already done. I've decided: we're staying here," Mike told him.

"Staying here? You mean in Hawaii? This is where you want your family laid to rest?" he questioned.

Mike was shaking his head, he was nervous and upset. "I don't want my wife or my baby laid to rest anywhere," he said angrily. I want them cremated and I want to release them to the sea that took them," he explained sternly.

"Oh." The priest was very surprised. "Aren't you Catholic?"

Mike looked him straight in the eyes. "This is what I want."

"Okay, son, I'll ask the hospital to start making the arrangements." The priest stood up and pulled his chair back. He walked back over to Mike and said a blessing.

"Father." Mike looked up at him. "Yes, Mike?" "I'm sorry it has to be this way." The priest nodded and walked out of the room.

Dumping human ashes into the sea in Hawaii is an illegal act, but the penalty only amounts to a ticket. Because Mike was one of their own, the local police and fire departments overlooked the infraction. Mike was driven by ambulance to the marina, and then helped onto a coastguard cutter with the box that contained his family's ashes. Mike told no one of the date and time this was going to happen, but all of his and Jessie's family and friends found out anyway. Mike did very little socializing with any of them: he couldn't even bear to look at Jessie's mother. Mike was the only one allowed on the cutter, the rest of the family and friends, including his fire chief, followed on a different boat. Mike wouldn't even allow the priest on the boat.

Fifteen minutes later they were stopped in the general area where the accident took place. Mike stood on the back of the boat by himself, holding the two urns under his arms. He removed the lids. In the other boat that was tethered to the cutter, everyone watched. The priest was saying a prayer out loud. Mike turned and looked at everyone on the other boat, stepped up to the edge of the platform, and dove into the water! Nearly everyone screamed. Five or six people from the two boats, including the fire chief, jumped in after him. Mike kicked as hard as he could with one leg. He swam deeper and deeper; his ears started to tighten up under the pressure, but he kept going. The ashes flowed from the urns. Mike was trying to get deep enough so he wouldn't have enough air to get back to the surface. The urns were empty, and Mike could swim no deeper. He was about to pass out when someone grabbed him by the arm. Mike resisted but didn't have the strength. On the way up to the surface he tried to suck in as much water as possible. He was choking but his body rejected the attempt. When they got to the surface, Mike threw up and gasped for air. He floated on top of the water with his head hanging down low. He was being helped by two coastguards, his chief and the priest.

Mike was moved from the general hospital to a psychiatric ward. He refused visitors, not even his family. He said nothing to anyone. He just lay there for days and days. His family couldn't wait around anymore, they had to get back home. Mike's mother and Jessie's mother begged the doctors and nurses to convince Mike to come back with them; he said nothing. He never even opened his eyes when they were in the room. They relayed their love and goodbyes, then left. In a note, Mike's chief told Mike to take as much time as he needed, he would always have a job for him when he returned. Mike got what he wanted: he was alone.

A few days later, the hospital had no choice, they had to release him. With only the clothes he had on from the day of the accident, and one photo of his wife and daughter posing on the beach in his pocket, he walked out of the hospital, straight for the beach. He threw his crutches in the trash on the way. There he sat for three days, without moving, without eating or drinking, just staring at the photo of his wife and child. It wasn't until he got rousted by a policeman that he finally got up and started to limp along the beach. Nowhere to go, he just kept walking.

Jono was released from the hospital to no fanfare. Maxwell set it up to look like Jono had left the day before and was already on a flight back to Los Angeles; no one was looking for her. At one point there were hundreds of photographers, television crews and reporters stalking the hospital and the hotel, hoping to catch a glimpse of the supermodel who nearly drowned. Maxwell checked out of the hotel they were staying in on the day Jono 'left', and checked them into a different hotel under a different name. Barely in the lobby, Jono went directly to the bar, and Maxwell went up to the room to start packing. Jono sat at a table by herself, covered by a hat and sunglasses: she was not recognized.

Jono was tall, very tall, just under five foot ten inches. Slender from head to toe. Long, blonde hair that reached two-thirds the way down her back. Razor blue eyes, perfect nose, high cheekbones, she was from a mold where there was only one. Jono was a spoiled, loud, demanding person. She expected everyone to jump when she asked. She was waited on hand and foot, every day, all day. She had a small staff who went with her everywhere; a personal assistant, a hair and make-up person, a nutritionist, a massage therapist, a personal trainer and of course her only real friend and manager, Maxwell.

Jono sat at her table sipping on her drink. This was the first tropical drink she'd ever had, recommended by the bartender. She really enjoyed it. She reflected on the previous three days, *What a disaster.* She thought a great deal about the story Maxwell told her about the events on the night of the party. She'd tried many times to force some kind of memory, but nothing came to her. Still the only thing that stuck like glue was the moment when Troy struck her. "Asshole," she mumbled.

Apparently, before Jono's boyfriend left the island he tried to take credit for saving her life, even the media didn't believe him. Maxwell reluctantly told Jono the name of her real hero, and with great effort tried to have him located. No one knew him or where he was: after he walked out of the courthouse he disappeared. Jono couldn't get this man out of her head. She wanted to talk to him, she wanted to thank him. Maxwell came and sat down at the table with Jono. "All set. I've got us on an 8:00 am flight tomorrow," he told her. She looked at him and smiled. "What would I ever do without you?" she said sincerely. Maxwell smiled. "Not much," he joked. "Boy, ain't that the truth?" she chuckled.

"We can't go home yet," she abruptly announced to Maxwell. His face went from a smile to a frown.

"Oh no, what is this?" he questioned.

"I can't leave until I ask this Mike Johnson some questions. I need to thank him, I need to apologize for the ape, and then I need to properly compensate him for saving my life!" she said determinedly.

"Jono, I love you, I would do anything for you, but this is a wild-goose chase. I've had so many people looking for him: if the guy doesn't want to be found, he won't be found."

"I know. You told me this already. But *I* haven't looked yet." She smiled coyly at Maxwell.

"Oh crap. Really? We're doing this?"

"We're not going home till it happens." She smiled as she took his hand.

"It's a damn good thing I love you," Maxwell said, giving in to Jono's request or demand.

"I love you, too. Now extend our stay and get us unpacked, will you? I'm starving!" She smiled with her little demeaning 'I'm-the-boss' look. "Yes, ma'am."

Maxwell Whistler, 'Max' to only Jono, had been Jono's manager and friend from the very beginning. He was a big man, physically and in the world of fashion. He was six foot three inches tall, weighed around two hundred and twenty-five pounds, *husky,* he called it and he sported a large, hairy, barrel-shaped chest. He wore his salt-and-pepper hair short and neat. One of the most well-groomed and meticulous dressers you would ever meet. Maxwell took attire very seriously.

He grew up in the fashion world, born in New York City miles from the fashion district where his mother worked as a seamstress and his father as a warehouse manager. By the time Maxwell was ten, he could sew as well and as fast as his mother, something his father was not proud of. He was fascinated with the materials; he was captivated by the process of taking different materials, putting them together and producing such beautiful and glamorous clothing. When he was sixteen, he was invited to his first fashion show by a designer he had helped. Maxwell was transfixed, but unlike most men, or fashionistas, he was more interested in the materials, how they were used, the models, how the clothes were worn, and how the clothing looked on the human form.

Maxwell tried on many hats in the fashion industry; he tried designing, which was a disaster; sales, marketing, layout, anything that would keep him in the business he knew he had to be in. Nothing was working, or working well. He was successful in everything he tried, except for designing, but he didn't like any of it. At twenty-four he was starting to feel he should consider looking into other things. As much as he loved fashion, he wasn't finding his niche.

At a major fashion show during fashion week in New York, Maxwell was asked by a designer friend to help out. Last-minute fittings, clothing layout, accessories, putting it all together for a great show. An hour before the show was to start, two models were going at it, a major catfight, only in two thousand-dollar dresses. The fight over make-up was quickly halted, but not after both dresses were damaged, and both models were ready to walk out. The designer's team, including Maxwell, jumped in and started working on repairs. The models continued yelling at each other, then in a hissy fit they both started for the door. Maxwell knew that, if they walked, not only would it put the designer and his show in jeopardy, but also these two well-known models would be blackballed from the industry. No one would ever take a chance on them again.

Maxwell jumped up and ran to the door, blocking it with his large presence. The models stopped and stared him down, but Maxwell wouldn't move. "I've got an idea," he told them. He took them both by the hand and together they went into the ladies' room, the only private place around. They were in there for ten minutes before they finally emerged, all smiling and giggling. The show was on, the models were happy, the designer was ecstatic. "What did you say to them?" he asked Maxwell. "Not much, really. I think I was able to help them see the big picture. That's all." The show went on without a hitch. By the end of the show Maxwell knew exactly what he wanted to do; he was a natural at dealing with these girls, he loved them all, thought of them as his friends, now he would manage them. Within a week he had six clients: you can guess who the first two to sign on were.

Maxwell was in his late-thirties when he and Jono first met. He discovered Jono purely by accident when she was thirteen. He spotted her walking through a mall with a group of her friends. Maxwell was immediately struck by this young girl's natural beauty. She had long, blonde hair tied in a ponytail; she was tall and thin, and her blue eyes were mesmerizing. Jono stood out to Maxwell, not only because she was a foot taller than her friends, but even through her baggy clothes, ugly hat and flip-flops he saw something, something he liked. It was difficult to approach her without coming across as creepy, but Maxwell was determined: there was no way he wasn't going to try. When Jono and her friends sat down at a table in the food court, Maxwell decided this would be his only chance. He introduced himself and handed out a few cards, but his focus was on Jono. Up close she was even more beautiful. There were a great deal of giggles, and a couple of the girls got up and left right away: Jono didn't. Her face told it all: if this was true and Maxwell wasn't some kind of pervert, she was interested.

Convincing Jono that day in the mall that she should consider modeling was effortless; convincing the evil mother was another matter. Maxwell tried several times, all with the same result, being thrown out of the house with the front door slammed behind him. Maxwell wanted this, and now Jono wanted this. In a final attempt, for now, Maxwell showed up at the house with an expensive bottle of Scotch in his hand. Jono's mother started to heel until Maxwell offered the bottle to her. She agreed to at least listen. Maxwell and Jono's mom sat on the couch drinking the Scotch; Jono was sent to her room. After a couple of hours of hard drinking, laughing and yelling, Jono's mom signed the contract allowing Maxwell to become her legal guardian and manager. Within hours they were on a plane headed for Los Angeles.

Maxwell was well aware that Jono was his creation, the good and the bad. He was not a father, and never would be but he was a good manager. Over time they became friends and did everything together. Jono never went anywhere without Maxwell. Maxwell treated Jono like a queen, even to the point of it working against him. He knew that she knew she was his boss, but over and above anything else they were friends, and they only trusted each other. Maxwell's whole life became Jono: her success grew so quickly he had no choice but to drop any other clients and only work with her. Jono always had her suspicions, but it wasn't until she was fifteen that Maxwell admitted to her that he was a gay man. Ever since, Jono had worked tirelessly to find Maxwell a boyfriend. Maxwell just laughed it off: "Sorry, honey, no time for anyone else but you!" But it didn't keep her from trying.

Jono and Maxwell walked up and down the beach for days, asking everyone they came across, locals and tourists alike, if they knew of, or had seen, Mike Johnson. No one had even heard of him. Jono was handing out money left and right looking for answers, but no solid leads. One evening the two of them, exhausted from their detective work, sat on the beach to watch the sunset. "Beautiful, isn't it?" Maxwell asked. "It is." Jono smiled.

"Excuse me, lady," a middle-aged man with a baseball cap and tethered clothes approached. "Great, here's another one." Maxwell referred to the word on the beach that Jono was giving away money with no strings. "Shhh," Jono insisted.

"Are you the lady looking for the fireman?" the man asked. Jono and Maxwell stood up. Jono looked at Maxwell. "Are we?" Maxwell lifted his shoulders in doubt. "I don't know."

"Well, is he or isn't he?" the bum asked impatiently.

"Yes, I believe we are." Jono thought it might be worth a shot. Maxwell looked at her then back at the obviously homeless man.

"Okay... five bucks." The man demanded, holding out his hand.

"Five dollars?" Jono asked. "I'll tell you what. If I feel the information you give me is good, I'll give you one hundred dollars!" The man's eyes nearly came out of his head. Maxwell said nothing. The bum sat down on the sand just in front of them. Jono and Maxwell sat down. He explained more about what he had heard than what he knew, but filled them in on Mike the fireman as best he could remember. He told them he had heard Mike was a fireman from the mainland who came to Hawaii some two years ago with his family on a vacation. He told them as much as he knew about Mike's tragic story. Even though he didn't know all of the details, they got the gist of it.

"Oh my God, that's just terrible!" Jono reacted. Maxwell was shaking his head in disgust. "What a terrible thing to happen, it's just so sad." Jono continued. "No wonder he's given up on life. I understand why he hasn't ever left here… he can't. This is just tragic. All the more reason we need to find him Max. This is important!" Maxwell agreed.

"What does he look like?" Maxwell asked. Maxwell only saw him briefly on the night of the party, plus it was dark, but he did have a description from the police department.

"Uh, well, he's really tall, he has long, junky, dark hair… oh and a beard. Nasty one." Maxwell was nodding as the bum continued. "He has on some torn-up blue shorts and a ripped-up old white tee shirt. I've never seen him with anything else. Kind of a strange guy, he never talks to anyone, pretty much stays to himself."

"How do you know so much about him?" Jono asked the man.

"Well, one day I was being bullied by some local kids, they were kicking and punching me, pushing me around, you know. Then this guy just shows up out of nowhere and scares them off. He didn't even have to touch them. When I tried to thank him, he walked off. But a police officer saw the whole thing, he's the one who told me his name and he told me his story."

Maxwell smiled at Jono. "This sounds like our guy." Jono agreed and gave the bum one hundred dollars. His face lit up like a child on Christmas morning.

"Have you seen him recently? Do you know where he is?" She asked as the bum started to walk away.

"I can't say for sure but I've seen him a lot over at the Village, I think he likes it there." Jono and Maxwell looked at each other. "The Village?" Jono smiled. The Village was where Dan's house was where the party was. A very upscale exclusive neighborhood, only for the rich and famous.

"Thank you!" The bum waved as he walked away.

"Didn't someone look there already? Didn't we?" Jono asked Maxwell.

"Yeah, several times, you know the ol' back to the scene of the crime thing."

"Well we're checking again. Come on!" Jono demanded.

"I guess we are."

By the time Jono and Maxwell got to the Village community it was very late. They walked the beach up and down in front of Dan's house and a great deal further in both directions. Nothing. They even rummaged around the outside of Dan's house to see if he might be hiding there. It was a little rough to see anything without a flashlight, and only the shine of the moon to go by. "I think we came a little unprepared!" Maxwell suggested. Jono was getting frustrated.

Maxwell, you go back to the hotel, get us some food and some flashlights. I'm just going to sit here and wait, I'm exhausted."

"Uh... no. I'm not leaving you out here all alone, bad idea. Why don't we both call it a night and we'll get a fresh start in the morning," he strongly suggested.

"Uh... no. I'm not moving." She sounded like a spoiled child. Maxwell knew there was no dealing with her when she was in this state, especially when she was tired. "Please, Maxwell?" she begged. Maxwell was a little stunned: he couldn't remember the last time Jono ever used *Please*, let alone begged. *She must be really tired!* "Fine!" Maxwell hurriedly walked off the beach toward the street. He yelled back to her, "Don't you move!" Jono waved her hand in agreement. She was too tired to move anyway.

Jono did move a little. She moved closer to the water to watch the waves. She threw her sandals down and plopped onto the sand next to them. Suddenly out of the corner of her eye she saw a shadow: Jono screamed and jumped to her feet. She turned to face the shadow, ready to run. "Sorry, I didn't mean to scare you," the male figure said. Jono stood stone-cold for several seconds, and the man smiled. "You're not thinking about going swimming again, are you?" he asked. In the moonlight she could see he was a tall man, with long, dark hair and a dark, unmanaged beard. "Are you Mike?" she asked, still keeping her distance. The man didn't answer. Jono started looking for someone to run to, but no one else was on the beach. The man sat down on the sand, making himself less dangerous. "Are you Mike?" Jono insisted. Mike nodded his head, "Yes." Jono couldn't believe it: after all the searching, he just shows up.

"Are you the one?" she asked stepping a little closer. Mike never lifted his head. "Are you the guy who pulled me out of the ocean and saved my life?" she pleaded. Jono was strangely overcome with emotions. Her heart was racing, her eyes welled up, and she dropped to her knees. "I'm sorry, I'm not trying to hurt you or bother you. I don't want to intrude in your life... but if it is you, I couldn't leave until I thanked you," she explained to him. Mike lifted his head to look at her. "Yes." He smiled again. He had a very nice smile - sincere, Jono thought.

"It was you! Oh my God, I can't believe it. You saved my life, you're my hero!" she said excitedly. Mike didn't like that at all; he looked around to see if anyone may have heard her.

"I'm no hero," he said with a degree of anger in his voice.

"Well, I don't care what you say, you're a hero to me!" she told him in the way only Jono can. Mike reluctantly smiled again. Jono sat down on the sand, still keeping some distance.

"Okay, I know that your name is Mike. My name is Jono." She reached out her hand. Mike hesitated then reached up and shook

Jono's hand. Mike's hand was very rough: hard, Jono noticed. "I don't know what to say but I feel like I need to talk to you. Would that be alright with you?" Jono smiled at him. Mike started to get up, and Jono lunged forward. "No! Please don't go!" She pleaded, grabbing his arm. Mike turned back. He wanted to resist, he wanted to leave; some strong feeling was forcing him to stay, so he sat back down.

"Thank you. Thank you so much. This means a lot to me." Mike nodded. "Here's the thing… I don't think just thanking the man who saved my life is enough," she started. "I'd like to do something for you. I know there is nothing I can do that could ever repay you or could ever express my sincere gratitude, but I really want to do something for you. Maybe I can help you somehow?" She didn't want to just come out and say it, the man is a bum. She thought anything she did for him would be a serious gesture.

"I'm fine. I don't need anything. I don't want anything," he told her, back to his angry voice.

"I'm so sorry, I'm not trying to offend you, really, I just want to help. I owe you a debt that I…" She was cut off.

"No you don't. It's fine, I'm fine. You owe me nothing, I was just doing my job," he said sternly.

"Your job?" she questioned, but knew exactly what he was talking about. "That's right, someone mentioned you are a fireman. Is that true?" she asked politely.

"Was."

"Was… well, thank God for that! If you weren't on the beach that night, I wouldn't be here with you now. Thank you for being there." Jono reached out and picked up his hand. It made Mike very uncomfortable; he slowly pulled his hand back. "Mike, is there anything I can do for you? A place to sleep, some new clothes, some money? That's it, can I give you some money to help you out? Then you can get whatever you need," she asked excitedly.

In a very somber, low tone Mike responded. He looked really upset. "No. Thank you, I'm fine." With that Mike stood up and started walking away. Jono quickly stood up. She thought about following him, but immediately changed her mind. "Wow!" She sat back down on the beach. Minutes later she could hear Maxwell calling her. "Jono! Where are you?" *Damn that girl, I told her to stay put!* "I'm here!" She yelled. Maxwell ran up to her with two big bags in his hands, breathing heavily.

"You weren't supposed to move!" he scolded her.

"I know, I just wanted to be closer to the water," she explained.

"Fine." Maxwell sat down and starting pulling out the contents of the bags. "I've got food here, some wine and a little dessert," he smiled. "Oh, and the hotel gave me these flashlights." He turned one on and shone it down the beach. "Good ones," he thought.

"Thank you, Max, but we won't be needing those anymore." Maxwell was confused, and his face showed it.

"Uh, okay. Why?"

"Let's eat, I'm starving." Jono smiled, and Maxwell shook his head in confusion.

Together they sat on the beach, eating and drinking wine while Jono told Maxwell everything that happened while he was gone. Maxwell was, to put it mildly, blown away.

"He just showed up?" He repeated what Jono told him. "I knew I shouldn't have left you by yourself! Who knows what could have happened!" he told her.

"Maxwell, really? Do you think the guy who saved me three days ago was going to have a change of heart and hurt me?" she scoffed.

"No, I guess you're right. But still!" he said, defending his position. "So I guess that's it then. You met your hero, thanked him... So I can book our flight home now, right?" Jono turned and looked at him and smiled. Maxwell knows that smile. "Jono, the man is a loner, a beach bum. He saved your life, yes, but I'm pretty sure he wants to be left alone. You know what I mean?" Maxwell pleaded more than asked.

"I know. You're right. But that's not what we're going to do. I've got to stay, I know I can help this man. He deserves it. And if not me, who? We're staying till I can figure this out." She smiled coyly. Maxwell unwillingly smiled back.

"Well, crap. Give the wine back!" Maxwell demanded with a smirk on his face. Jono smiled and handed him the bottle of wine. "Thanks, Max."

UNEXPECTED ANGEL

Jono barely slept that night thinking about Mike and his tragic life. *How can I help this man?* She was determined to help him somehow, even if he didn't want to be helped. So many different ideas went through her mind: none of them made sense. She knew if she was too aggressive he would run, and she'd never find him again. *What can I do?* She thought about bringing him some new clothes, maybe some food; what she really wanted to do was give him enough money to lift him up out of his state in life. She knew *Mike the fireman* would never take money: *He made that clear enough. There has to be a way.* She knew if he wouldn't take money, she had to figure out a different way.

"Good morning!" Maxwell said with a spring in his step as he entered Jono's room. Because Jono was on the lam, she had to lay low as much as possible, so she and Maxwell with a few exceptions only ate in her room.

"Good you're here. Breakfast just got here. Sit down, I think I have a plan." She smiled.

"Oh no," Maxwell responded in a serious tone.

"Quiet..." she teased. "I thought about it all night. The guy's just not going to let me walk up to him and hand him some money or clothes... or anything. He wants to be alone and stay alone. I wonder what he eats?" she questioned, cutting herself off. Maxwell shrugged. "Fish, I guess."

"Mike is, or was, a fireman, right?" She was speaking out loud.

"Right."

"What do firemen do?" she asked in an excited voice.

"Put out fires?" Maxwell joked: he knew where she was going. Jono didn't smile. "Help people." He grinned. "Is that what you want me to say?" he asked sharply.

"Yes, they help people. We've got to come up with an idea that forces him to do what he naturally does, and somehow pay him for it." She was shaking her head as she heard her own words. "Yeah, that's not going to work," she admitted.

"Can't we just take him a briefcase full of money and walk away? If he doesn't want it, so be it: there will be plenty of other happy beach bums that day!" Maxwell laughed.

"Maxwell... this is not funny. This is making me nuts, I can't think about anything else, I've got to help Mike." She was very serious. Maxwell knew he had to help, somehow. Otherwise they were never going to leave the island.

"Hey! I've got an idea!" Maxwell chirped excitedly.

"Just like that. You've got an idea?" Jono questioned.

"I do!"

"Okay... so?"

"Mike, our beach bum friend and hero, likes to hang out around the Village, right?"

"Right."

"Let's call Dan and get his house!"

"Oh my God, that's brilliant!" Jono jumped up excitedly. "Then we can be nearby, we can watch and learn, I don't have to hide, and we can eat some decent food! Maxwell, this is great!"

Maxwell was shaking his head, puffing out his chest. It was always a good day when Jono called you 'brilliant'.

In a little over an hour they were out of the hotel and standing in front of Dan's house. Jono was super-excited. The live-in house-keeper and cook Kaleen greeted them at the door. "Aloha, welcome." "Aloha," Jono greeted her back. She and Maxwell entered the house. "Oh my God, it's so beautiful!" Jono exclaimed. "Oh, and look at that view!" She practically ran to the other side of the room and out onto the deck. "Max! This is so beautiful!" Max chuckled as he walked up to her.

"What?" Jono smiled.

"You don't remember... Do you?"

Jono looked around then went back inside the house where she looked around some more.

"No. I don't," she said lowering her head. "Not a thing." She plopped herself down on one of the beautiful, oversized sofas. Maxwell came and sat down next to her. Kaleen emerged from the kitchen with a tray of food and drinks. "A little something until dinner," she offered. "Oh Kaleen, that looks fantastic." Jono was truly impressed. The 'snack' consisted of an array of perfectly sliced fruits, put together in a beautiful display. Pineapple, mango, papaya and coconut wedges. Then there were three different kinds of cheeses with crackers and bread, plus a small bowl of chocolate-covered macadamia nuts. "I know what I'm starting with," Maxwell announced, picking up the bowl of chocolates.

Kaleen also put out a pitcher of what looked like tea, but was an off-white color. "Kaleen, what's this drink?" Jono asked as politely as she could.

"Oh, that's my own home-made tea, I hope you like it. Please let me know if there is anything else I can do or get you. It's important that your stay here is perfect." She slipped away into another part of the house.

"Wow... perfect." Jono smiled.

"That's got 'Dan' written all over it," Maxwell said as he stuffed his second handful of nuts into his mouth.

"This is something I could get used to!" Jono got up and walked back out onto the deck. "Do you think he's out there?" Jono asked as Maxwell came out and stood next to her.

"He is. Somewhere. Don't worry, we'll figure this out. But in the meantime, why don't we… you and I, have a little fun?!" he said excitedly. Jono smiled and clapped her hands.

"The beach?"

"The beach!" Maxwell and Jono raced back into the house.

Jono had been all over the world: she had stood on some of the most amazing beaches in the world, some of which only a handful of Westerners had ever seen. There was something about where she was now that was different for her. The beach had beautiful, white, silky sand, the waves were a rainbow of different shades of blue, and the palm trees and plants covered in flowers seemed as if they were painted in place. The warm, tropical breeze was moving the spellbinding aromas all around her. She lay back on her towel, and in an instant fell asleep. Was it because of where she was? Or maybe it was not being pushed in thirty directions every second of every day, or, more likely, a satisfaction of completion, finding her hero. Truly for the first time in many years, Jono found herself accidentally on vacation. She was discovering a new peace she didn't know was possible.

Jono was nudged awake by Maxwell. "What is it?" she asked.

"Treats."

Jono sat up: standing right next to her was a small, older, Hawaiian man. "Aloha."

"Aloha to you." Maxwell smiled.

"My name is Kale. I'm Kaleen's husband and the keeper of the house. Welcome to Hawaii. The wife thought you might like something to eat and drink." He set down the beautiful tray of food and drinks.

"Oh good, more tea! Please tell Kaleen thank you very much and tell her I love her tea, it's amazing!"

"I'm so glad you like it, and I will." Kale turned and walked back toward the house.

"Seriously, Max… I think this might be a little slice of Heaven." After sipping some tea she lay back down. Maxwell wasn't sure how to react, he'd never seen Jono like this before, not even when she was a kid. He, too, took a sip of the tea and lay down.

Every day and every night, Jono and Maxwell walked the beach looking for Mike. They had no idea what they would say or do, they just wanted to find him again. Even with all the searching, they did manage to have some fun. They went swimming several times a day, both in the ocean and in the pool; they ate like royalty, Kaleen made sure of that, and they relaxed: a very big deal for both of them. Jono even started a book: unheard of. Early in the mornings Jono would get up and go out on the deck. With binoculars from the house (likely used by Dan for bikini watching) Jono would scour the beach for Mike. Three days had passed: not a single sighting. Jono was getting frustrated. Maxwell didn't care as much anymore, he was enjoying the much-needed break and the chocolate macadamia nuts.

"I really thought he'd be here," Jono said.

"Yeah, me, too. I'm sorry, honey, I don't know what else we can do," Maxwell told her.

Jono nodded in frustration. "Maybe it's time to think about going home."

"I think that's probably the right thing to do. We tried. I know this is not what you were hoping for, but we really should get back," Maxwell suggested.

"Okay, but another couple of days, alright? Let's wait till Saturday."

"No problem. I'll schedule the flight."

"In the meantime, let's go swimming!" Jono pushed Maxwell hard on his chest.

"Sounds good to me!" Maxwell laughed, chasing behind her.

Maxwell was sitting on the beach, up close to where the waves were breaking. He was enjoying some of Kaleen's tea and munching on some fresh pineapple when Jono came up to him with a large surfboard she could barely carry in tow. "What is that, and what are you doing with it?" he half-joked.

"It's a surfboard and I'm going surfing!" Jono laughed.

"Surfing? You're messing with me, right?" Maxwell's voice got a little more serious.

"No, I'm not. Hey, we're in Hawaii, we're leaving in a couple of days… I've got to at least try it." She started for the water.

"Jono, I don't think this is a very good idea," he yelled, running behind her. *Man, this girl!* "Jono! I need you to stop. Let's talk about this… please?" Jono didn't slow down even a little. She laid the board on top of the foamy, shallow water and lay down on top of it. Maxwell ran into the water right behind her, reached out and grabbed the back of the board. "Jono, what the heck are you doing? You trying to kill yourself for a second time?" he asked, scolding her quite bluntly.

"No, I'm not trying to kill myself. I just want to try, that's all. Look, I promise I won't go out very far, I'll stay on these baby waves. It'll be fun!" she tried to convince him. "Now let go!" she demanded. Maxwell let go of the board. Jono impressively paddled out past the small breaks and into slightly deeper water. She struggled but eventually got the surfboard turned around and then she sat up. *Now where'd she learn to do that?* Maxwell was astonished. Within seconds a small wave was headed her way. She lay back down and paddled like a crazy woman trying to catch the wave. The wave rolled right under her, passing her by. "Damn!"

She paddled back out, a little further this time. "This is all about timing, I can do this." she told herself. "Here's one!" She had to quickly paddle to her right and get into position. She turned the board toward shore and paddled with all her arms could give. Next thing she knew she was gliding along with the wave! She lay there screaming her head off: "Max! Look at me!" A total rush. Ten seconds later she was at Maxwell's feet.

"Did you have fun? Can you stop now?" he asked.

"Are you kidding? That was amazing! I'm going again!" She turned the surfboard back toward the ocean, jumped on it and paddled back out. This time she went even further out, Maxwell yelling at her that she was going too far had no effect. She spotted a wave that was starting to form: this time she had to move to her left, and so she turned the board toward the beach and started paddling. This wave was a little larger, it grabbed her like she was a toothpick and rushed her toward the beach. Jono was screaming her head off. Then, seconds later, the nose of the surfboard dipped under the wave and flipped Jono into the water. Maxwell yelled and started to swim in her direction. He couldn't see her, and he started to panic. "Jono!" He stood in waist-deep water, spinning in circles. "Jono!" He turned out toward the water, looking in every direction, "Ouch! What the hell was that?!" he yelled. Out popped Jono from the foam of the water. She leaped into Maxwell's arms. "Oh my God! That was so much fun!" she screamed into his ear. Maxwell let out an audible sigh of relief. "Good time for a break, don't you think?" "Sure." Jono retrieved the surfboard, and Maxwell helped her carry it out of the water.

SURFING LESSON

Jono was exhausted but she was having a blast. She and Maxwell sat on the beach enjoying some more of Kaleen's treats, laughing and talking. Jono was on an adrenaline rush. She tried but, no matter what she said, she wasn't going to convince Maxwell to give it a try. "Swimming, yes... surfing, no." He laughed. They lay on their towels continuing to talk; the sun was sitting low on the western horizon, then a shadow blocked their sun. Jono and Maxwell sat up quickly. The sun was in their eyes, but they couldn't see who it was. Jono thought it must be Kale. Maxwell thought the worse, that the paparazzi must have discovered Jono. "Hi," came a man's voice. He moved out of the sunlight toward their feet. It was Mike.

"Mike!" Jono yelped as she stood up. "It's so good to see you... I can't believe you're here, but I'm so happy you are." Maxwell cleared his throat as he stood. "Oh, where are my manners? Mike, this is my manager and best friend, Maxwell."

"It's a pleasure, Mike, an honor really," Maxwell told him sincerely as he reached out to shake his hand. Mike nodded and shook Maxwell's hand. "Thank you."

"So, Mike…" Jono got a little flustered. "Wow, you're here. I was hoping to see you again before I had to go," she explained.

"Go? Home?" he asked.

"Yes, Maxwell and I are headed back to LA on Saturday. I've got to get back to work, you know: can't be on vacation all of the time!" She smiled.

"I am," Mike said bluntly, completely throwing off both Jono and Maxwell. Then he smiled.

"Oh yeah, right. I get it!" Maxwell laughed.

"Mike, would you like to sit with us and have a little something to eat? I promise you, you'll hate yourself if you don't at least try Kaleen's home-made macadamia nut cookies." She smiled invitingly.

"Maybe for a minute." Jono looked at Maxwell with an *I can't believe this* face. Maxwell gave it right back to her. Jono sat first, then Maxwell, then Mike sat between them with his back to the water. Maxwell offered the tray of cookies to Mike: he took one off of the tray and looked at it. "I haven't seen one of these in a while," he admitted. Neither Jono nor Maxwell had any idea how to respond, so they sat quietly and watched Mike take the first bite. He smiled with approval. "You're right. I would have hated myself." Jono chuckled, Maxwell smiled.

"Is that from the other night?" Jono asked Mike, pointing at his black eye. Mike nodded. "That asshole. I am so sorry, my stupid ex-boyfriend. He's an idiot!"

"Don't hold back or anything." Maxwell indicating Jono was going a little overboard.

"Yeah, sorry. I'm pretty pissed off about the whole thing. Anyway, I'm sorry and I hope you're okay?" she asked in a calmer tone.

"I'm fine."

Finally Jono got to see what Mike really looked like. Other than a few minutes in the dark, Maxwell's accounts, and her dreams, she really had no idea. Jono expected Mike to be thin, malnourished-looking. He wasn't. She was first struck by his body: *Oh my God!* she reacted to herself. He was slender with surprisingly muscular arms and a big chest that looked like the tee shirt was having difficulty keeping in. *Huge!* Jono smiled, not realizing she was gawking. Very athletic-looking. His eyes are a deep, dark brown, large and clear, even with the bad bruising. This surprised her. He was tall, like she had been told: she guessed six foot three or four. His hair was dark and hung down to his shoulders: it looked shorter than she remembered from a few nights ago. He had it combed back off his face, not as nasty as she thought it would be. His beard was long, unmanaged, inconsistent and, well, terrible-looking. He was much younger than Jono thought he would be. She wasn't sure but thought he might be in his early to mid-thirties.

For a few long seconds there was an awkward silence. Maxwell spoke up first. "So Mike, how long have you lived here in Hawaii?" he asked. Jono gave Maxwell a dirty look, Mike caught it, then smiled.

"About two and a half years now. I love it here, my life is here," he told them.

"You know, I've been to Hawaii many times before, but it wasn't until this trip that I got it. I finally see. This is an amazing place," Jono told Mike.

"Yes it is." He nodded supportively. "I've been coming here since I was a teen, then I finally moved here to stay," he explained.

"Do you surf?" was the only question Maxwell could think of that shouldn't get him in trouble with Jono.

"Yes, I do." Mike's face lit up a little. "I've been surfing since I was around ten, it gives me peace," he told them. "I saw you do a little surfing," Mike said, smiling at Jono.

"You saw that? Oh well, in my defense, that was the first time I ever tried," she embarrassingly explained.

"Really? Your first time? That wasn't bad," Mike told her.

"Wasn't bad? You're teasing me, right? I was terrible!"

"Not really. If that was your first time ever, you've already got all you need to get up on a board and really surf."

"You're kidding." Maxwell didn't mean to say it out loud. Jono laughed. "Thanks!"

"No, I'm not kidding. It can take someone a long time to figure out their balance, learn how and when to paddle out, and, most important, being able to judge the waves is the key to surfing. You did all of that."

"Hmm... I guess I did."

"Yeah, and when did you have time to learn this?" Maxwell asked, a little puzzled.

"Well... I've been watching the surfers out here for days, and I also caught a few surfing shows on TV," she explained. "I guess I am just naturally talented," she joked. Even Mike chuckled a little. Then the sound of the magical dinner bell rang out from the house. "Mike, it's dinner. Would you like to join us?" Jono asked in a begging way.

"No, no, I'm sorry, I can't stay." Mike stood up: Jono and Maxwell also stood. "Thank you very much, the cookie was great."

"Oh well, here, take them with you, there are plenty more of these in the house. And trust me, the last thing I need around the house is cookies!" Jono kidded. Mike accepted. He started to walk down the beach, toward the sunset. Jono was staring: she found herself daydreaming, admiring his body as he walked away, then he suddenly turned back, catching Jono off guard.

"Do you want to learn how to surf?" he yelled out. Maxwell looked at Jono.

"Yes. I mean Yes! I'd love to learn how to surf."

"I can teach you."

"Okay... that'd be great!"

Mike continued. "Meet me here at six tomorrow morning!" he yelled.

"Did he say six?" Maxwell asked.

"I think he did."

"Okay then, let me know how it goes!" Maxwell received a whack on the arm for that one.

At 6:01 in the morning Jono was wrapped in a white terrycloth robe, carrying two cups of coffee across the sand to the beach. Sitting on the beach looking out over the water was Mike; lying next to him was a very large surfboard, much larger than the one Jono used the day before. Jono was impressed: she wasn't sure if Mike would really be there, she was fully prepared to go back to bed. "Hi," she said as she got closer. Mike stood up and turned to greet her.

"Good morning." Jono handed Mike a cup of hot coffee. "Thanks. Are you ready to do this?" Mike asked after only one sip of his coffee.

"Sure. Why exactly are we doing this so early in the morning?" Jono had to ask.

"Look!" Mike pointed toward the ocean. Jono understood right away. The sea was smooth, the waves were clean and small, and there was no one around. Jono smiled. "Cool." She set down her coffee and dropped her robe; Mike literally took a step back. Jono had on a small, very sexy, black bikini, a suit only a body like hers could get away with.

"Oh man! Is this not appropriate! Should I go change?" Mike tried not to stare, but that was just not possible. "I wasn't sure what is considered surfing wear. I'll go change." She started to turn.

"No no. You're fine." Mike snapped out of it. "You'll be fine. Come on, lesson one." Jono smiled. She naturally expected that reaction.

"What's first?" Jono asked, stepping up to the board. "Wow, this thing is huge! It's more like a small boat."

"We call it a longboard. It will be easier for you to learn on, and hopefully stand on," Mike explained. Mike was struggling to keep his focus. "Lay down on the board, please," he instructed. "Sure. Oooh, a little cold." Mike just smiled.

"Now pretend you're paddling to catch a wave. When I tell you I want you to push off with your hands and spring straight to your feet, right here in the center of the surfboard. Keep your knees bent and your hands out at your side for balance. Now!" Mike yelled. Jono pushed off with her hands and sprung up to her feet all in one motion.

"TaDa!" Jono said proudly.

"Yeah, not bad. Let's do it a couple more times."

"Okay! This is fun!" Jono said with a great deal of excitement. Mike was trying hard not to laugh, so he smiled. He hadn't smiled much in the past couple of years. Jono made him laugh: it felt good, it gave him an unfamiliar warmth. After a few more practice tries, Mike decided Jono was ready for the real thing. He explained to her step-by-step exactly how it was going to work. "You're going with me, aren't you?" Jono asked in a nervous voice.

"I'll be with you every step of the way," he told her. "This is a big and heavy board: if you start to fall, jump away from it. You don't want to get hit by this thing," he emphasized.

"Got it. Jump away." Jono was nervous but really excited to prove to herself she could do this. Mike pulled off his tight, tethered tee shirt, threw it on the sand, picked up the surfboard, and started walking into the water. This time, Jono took a step back. *Wow!* she said to herself. He was cut like no other man Jono had ever seen, and she'd seen a few. His stomach was a tight washboard, his hairless chest almost square and so powerful-looking. His arms, Jono's weakness, were *perfect*. His whole body was covered in a glorious golden tan. Not what Jono expected at all; this was the second time Mike had caught her off guard. "Are you coming?" Mike called back. "Yeah…" she cleared her throat. "Yes!" She ran into the water to catch up. A lot cooler at six in the morning. Jono started to shiver.

"Are you going to be alright?" Mike knew the water was cooler than Jono expected: she really wasn't dressed for it, but Mike wasn't going to say anything.

"Yup, I'm good." But quietly her teeth were chattering. They got about waist-deep, and Mike held the board. "Okay, jump on!" Jono didn't hesitate and climbed on the board. A wave crashed over them. Jono held on, and Mike held the board securely, keeping it from taking off. *Okay, that was cold!* Jono said to herself. She started to paddle: a larger wave was about to crash over them. Mike, holding one side of the board with his left hand, jumped across Jono, laying his chest on her backside. Mike felt so warm to Jono; after the wave crashed over them he pushed himself back off of her into the water, leaving his right arm over her butt. For many seconds Jono stopped breathing. "You ready?" he asked. But before Jono could react, Mike pushed her hard, up and over the last of the breaking waves. Once in the smooth water, Jono sat up on the board.

"It's so beautiful out here." The water was calm, smooth like glass, the sun was still low in the east, and there were almost no sounds except the sound of the waves and her fast-beating heart. Mike could see in Jono's face she was absorbing all of it.

"Okay, here comes your first victim!" Mike yelped. Jono turned to look. She could see a small wave building, coming right at her. "Get yourself into position. I'll tell you when to start paddling." Jono watched the wave intently: her heart was pounding hard, and the cold she felt had gone. "Now!" Mike yelled. He pushed her hard and she paddled with everything she had. The board was gliding over the water pushed by the force of the developing wave: she caught it. "Now! Now!" Mike yelled from behind. Jono moved her hands in under her chest, then pushed hard and sprung up to her feet, all in one motion. She was standing! Mike couldn't hear what she was saying, but he was sure the screams were excitement. The whole ride lasted for only about three seconds. Jono celebrated a little too hard and lost her balance. She jumped away from the board as instructed and swam under the wave; she popped up seconds later. Mike swam to her.

"How was that?" he asked with a big smile.

"That was the most amazing thing I've ever done!" Jono punched the water with her fist. "Let's do it again!" she demanded. Mike started laughing. "What?" she asked him.

"You've got the bug already."

"I do? That's a good thing, right?" She smiled, wiping the sea water away from her face.

"That's a good thing." Mike was shaking his head, laughing as he went to shore to retrieve the surfboard. Another wave was breaking, and, like an old pro, Jono met it head-on and dove in under the base of the wave, coming out on the other side of it. "Nice!" Mike told her as he paddled up on the surfboard. He jumped off and Jono jumped on. Her second ride was a life-changing event for Jono. She spotted the wave, got into position, paddled on her own, and caught a nice little wave; she stood up almost immediately and rode the wave all the way to shore, screaming the entire time. Mike slapped the water out of excitement for her. He was proud, excited and impressed. He was attracted to her enthusiasm and determination. Her immediate reaction to surfing was remarkable. The way she appreciated and respected her surroundings was not natural for a mainlander. The way she treated Mike, the way she looked at him and made him smile: that wasn't natural either.

They surfed for another hour or so. Jono's arms felt like they were going to fall off. Mike carried the board in and set it down high up on the beach. "The tide's starting to come in," he explained.

Jono looked out over the water. "I see that." She sat down next to Mike, whose wet body was glistening in the sun. Jono took in a deep breath. "That was amazing: I have no words." She smiled at him.

"That's what true surfing is, it's as much a spiritual thing as it is fun and exciting." Jono was nodding her head in agreement. "I told you, this is how I get my peace."

"I understand. I..." Jono was abruptly interrupted.

"Hey, you two!" Maxwell came bouncing up to them with Kaleen following close behind. "Breakfast is served!" he announced proudly. Mike and Jono stood: Maxwell stopped dead in his tracks when he saw Mike. "Oh my God!" he blurted out. Jono whacked him on the shoulder. "Oh sorry, right. Okay, Kaleen and I have brought breakfast. I thought you guys would be hungry by now."

"I'm famished!" Jono spoke up first.

"I'd like to stay but I really should get going," Mike told them.

"What? Really? You have an important appointment you need to get to?" Jono asked, a little snippety. Then Kaleen spoke up. She said something in what Jono and Maxwell assumed was Hawaiian directly to Mike. Mike responded to her.

"Okay, I can stay for a little while." Mike sat down. Maxwell and Jono looked at Kaleen. She smiled, set down the enormous tray of food, and walked back to the house.

"Wow... that was... interesting," Maxwell said. "What did she say to you? I mean, if you don't mind me asking."

"She told me I needed to be more respectful of such an invitation. And she told me if I didn't eat her pancakes, she would hunt me down." Mike smiled. Both Jono and Maxwell laughed out loud. Together the three of them sat enjoying Kaleen's always amazing cooking.

"So how did our budding surfer do this morning?" Maxwell asked Mike.

"Really well. Remarkable, actually."

"Oh go on!" Jono jested. There was a pause. "No, I mean it: keep talking about how great I was. A natural, right?" It was funny, and Mike laughed pretty hard.

"So how about you?" Mike said to Maxwell. "You ready to give it a try?" he asked.

"Me? No... but thank you." He nervously smiled. Mike knew the answer, but thought it would be fun to ask.

They sat for some time enjoying each other's company and simple conversation. They talked about Hawaii and the surfing culture; they spoke about food, but no one got any deeper. Jono wanted to ask Mike so many questions but resisted. After they were done with breakfast, Jono asked Mike if they could go out again. "No no, not a good time. Take a look at those waves now, too big and choppy. It's way too rough out there."

"Awe, man. I was hoping to go again," Jono whined.

"Glass off," Mike said.

"Glass what?" Maxwell asked. Mike smiled.

"Glass off. It's the opposite of this morning. Right around sunset the water will get really calm again, as the tide recedes. It's a great time to go surfing."

"That sounds great!" She looked at Mike with her best pouty eyes. "Can we go again then?" Mike chuckled. "Sure." He smiled. "Meet me here just before sunset and we'll go again." Jono clapped with excitement.

"Perfect. This time I'll wear something a little more appropriate." She smiled. Mike nodded his head and smiled back. "Whatever works for you I'm sure will be fine." He didn't have an issue with what she was wearing, not even a little, but she was probably right.

"So, I'll see you guys then. Thank you for the breakfast: please tell Kaleen her pancakes were excellent." He smiled, picked up his tee shirt, and started down the beach.

Both Jono and Maxwell watched Mike walk away until he disappeared out of sight. "Okay! Who was that masked man?" Maxwell smiled.

"I know, right?" Jono agreed. "Wow! He's such a nice guy, you know… once I actually got him to talk."

"You not being able to make a man talk? Yeah right. Stutter at the least. But that's not exactly what I was talking about." Maxwell smirked.

"I know what you were talking about. Yes, he's got a pretty nice body. I wasn't really looking." Maxwell burst out laughing, rolling on his back. "Okay fine, maybe I looked a little." It didn't work, and Maxwell couldn't stop, causing Jono to start laughing with him. Once the laughing subsided, Maxwell sat back up and asked Jono: "So what did you learn?"

"Nothing. He didn't tell me a thing about himself or his life. Funny, though, he never asked about me either," she realized. They were so caught up in the surfing and having so much fun, it just never came up.

"That's kind of strange, isn't it?" Maxwell asked.

"Is it? I guess so. I mean we spent three hours together and the only thing I really know about him is he's a great surf teacher and he's a beach bum. Hmm, this is going to take some work." Maxwell laughed again. "What?"

"Oh nothing." Jono shoved Maxwell down onto his back and jumped onto his belly. She knew all the right spots and started tickling him feverishly. Maxwell laughed and laughed to the point of almost not breathing. Jono got off and let him go.

"Max."

"Yup?"

"I need you to cancel our flights."

"Yup."

NEXT LESSON

Jono was on pins and needles the rest of the day. She was so nervous and so excited, she had to take two showers. "What's wrong with you?" Maxwell asked curiously.

"I don't know? I'm nervous, I guess."

"Nervous? Honey, you've got this surfing thing down, you'll be fine. I'm actually looking forward to watching," Maxwell admitted.

"Naw. I'm not nervous about the surfing: that I'm excited about!"

"Well, what then?"

Jono turned and looked at Maxwell. "Oh. I see," Maxwell chuckled. "So you're nervous about seeing your fireman. You... nervous about meeting with a man? This is a first," he joked.

"Maxwell!" she snapped at him. "It's not funny. Mike's a good guy... He saved my life. I'm so confused. I still haven't figured out how I can help him," she said angrily. All the feelings, all the emotions were new territory for Jono, and Maxwell knew this.

"Well, first of all I'm pretty sure you filled your obligation to repay him."

"What do you mean? How?"

"Mike is not the man he was two days ago, and that's your doing."

"Awe, come on."

"Nope, it's one hundred percent true. And... whatever it is you think you're feeling, that's called the Nightingale syndrome."

"The what?" Jono was starting to pace the floor; the sun was quickly setting.

"It's when someone falls in love with their hero: it's very common."

"Love! Maxwell, what's wrong with you? Love, really! Oh crap, there he is!" Jono yelped seeing Mike walk up on the beach. "Come on, let's go!"

"Right behind you," Maxwell said calmly. He grabbed all their stuff, including a camera, and headed out to the beach.

"Hi!" Jono smiled.

"Hi. You look ready." Mike smiled. This time Jono and Maxwell went into town and picked up Jono some swim shorts and a rash guard tee shirt to go over her bikini top.

"Yeah, better, right?"

"Better? More appropriate maybe," he smiled. Jono nearly blushed. Maxwell came up and said hi. He set down their stuff and picked up the camera. "Is it okay if I take some pictures?" he asked Mike. Mike looked at Jono. Jono nodded.

"Okay with me," he told him. Jono and Mike ran for the water. "Wait. Wait!" Maxwell yelled. "Let me get a picture of you two before the hair disaster!" Jono and Mike posed on the beach just in the water. Mike put his arm around Jono's waist, giving her chills; she liked it. She smiled a little differently than she normally did when she was posing, and Maxwell picked up on it right away. *Hmmm...*, he thought to himself. Maxwell was going nuts taking pictures of everything as Jono entered the water and jumped on the surfboard. It didn't take long until Jono was up on her first wave, screaming and waving the entire way to the beach. Maxwell was standing knee-deep in the water, snapping off pictures as fast as the camera would allow him. The sun was setting fast; Maxwell started to get nervous for Jono. "Don't you think it's time to come in?" he asked one of the times she got close enough. "Now? No, Mom, soon," she teased.

Jono was the one doing all the surfing. With each wave she got better and better; she had some good wipe-outs but they didn't phase her at all. She'd hop right back on the board and paddle out to catch the next one. While she and Mike were out beyond the breaking waves waiting on the next ride, Jono noticed that Mike looked like he was getting tired. Each time he made sure Jono was safely away, he had to tread water the whole time until she would get back. "Mike, I'm so sorry. I'm so selfish."

"Why? What are you talking about?"

"You look exhausted… We should go in. I can't believe you've been out here all this time helping me, and you haven't ridden one wave."

"It's okay, I'm fine, just cramping up a little," he told her.

"Awe… that's it. We need to get in. I'm not going to let *you* drown after you saved me from drowning! Come on!" she demanded. Mike grabbed the board and stopped her. "What?"

"Can we go in together? I am getting pretty tired," he asked.

"Together? Sure. How do we do that?" she asked. With one powerful movement Mike pulled himself up on the board. He was lying on the surfboard, half on Jono with his feet hanging off the back, dangling in the water. Jono smiled, which Mike couldn't see.

"Are you okay?" Mike asked. She could feel the muscles in his arms flexing as he stroked the water.

"Oh yeah, I'm fine," she chirped.

"Mike started paddling harder; the board was moving much faster than it ever did when Jono was paddling. "Get ready!" Mike yelled.

"Ready for what?" she yelled back. Suddenly they were on a wave, rushing forward. She felt Mike moving around behind her, but was afraid to take her eyes off the water; suddenly a hand touched her on the back of her thigh. "Slowly get up!" Mike told her. "Get up?" she shrieked. She turned and looked back. Mike was standing right behind her, crouched down low. Jono carefully reached back with one hand, and Mike slowly guided her up to her feet. Next thing Jono realized, she and Mike were surfing together! Gliding smoothly across the wave, the sun nearly set, leaving behind a sky full of reds, oranges and purples: Jono was in Heaven. The board wobbled, Jono reached back and grabbed onto Mike's waist, and Mike pulled her back into him. Together they were holding their hands high in the air, Jono screaming at the top of her lungs. Maxwell was losing it he was so excited, snapping pictures like one of the paparazzi he hated so much. Then the ride was abruptly halted when the tip of the surfboard plunged under the water, causing Mike and Jono to fly off.

Maxwell shrieked, nearly dropping the camera in the water. Mike immediately resurfaced but Jono didn't. Maxwell screamed out, "Jono!" Mike dove under the water, then resurfaced: no Jono. "Jono!" Maxwell screamed again. Mike dove under the water again, right as a wave crashed down on him. Seconds later, Mike and Jono surfaced. "Oh thank God!" Maxwell yelled. Mike picked up Jono and carried her the rest of the way in. "You don't have to do this, I'm fine really," Jono told him. "I know. Old habits, I guess." Mike smiled, and Jono closed her eyes and rested her head on his chest.

"Is she okay?" Maxwell asked, running up to them.

"She's fine," Mike started, then Jono popped open her eyes, wrapped her arms around Maxwell's neck, and pulled him all the way into the water. Maxwell reached out with his camera and handed it to Mike just as he was about to submerge. Jono jumped onto Maxwell's back and together they romped around like little kids. Mike laughed and took pictures.

Back on the beach, the three of them sat and watched the last of the sun's rays disappear into the water; stars started to dot the sky. "Mike, you should stay for dinner," Maxwell told him.

"Oh." Mike lowered his head. You could tell he was thinking.

"Maxwell, brilliant as usual. I'm sorry, Mike, I won't take no for an answer. It is the least I can do for the fabulous surfing lessons and...

you know, for saving my life!" she joked. Maxwell laughed. Mike looked at Maxwell then at Jono. "Is Kaleen cooking?" He smiled. Jono whacked him on the shoulder. "Come on! I'm starving!" Jono jumped to her feet and ran for the house. Mike and Maxwell followed.

"Is she always like this?" Mike asked. Maxwell looked at Mike, trying to size up the question. He paused for a long time.

"No. She's never like this. Only when she's around you." Maxwell smiled at him. Mike smiled but did not respond.

They each went to their own bathroom to clean up after a full day at the beach. Jono started singing while she was in the shower: Maxwell could hear her from three rooms away. He started laughing, then started humming along. Mike stood naked in his shower with no water for a number of minutes, trying to figure out how to turn it on. There were plenty of nozzles and buttons but nothing seemed to work. He was about to get out when he noticed a wall switch right outside the shower. He flipped it on: *whoosh!* water was streaming out in front of him, behind him and over his head. He felt like he was in a hurricane. He couldn't help but laugh. After a few minutes, however, he really started liking it. An exceptional experience most people, not just him, get to try. It was awesome. By the time he was done in the shower he couldn't see three inches in front of him, there was so much steam. "Too hot, I guess." Mike wiped away the condensation from the giant mirror. He stood there looking at himself, staring into his own eyes. He could see so much hurt. Memories flooded his mind, and his eyes started to well up. He caught himself, then he got angry. He turned on the cold water in the sink and splashed his face. He opened a drawer to see if he could find a comb or brush. The cabinets had everything anyone could need and more.

Jono and Maxwell were sitting out on the deck, having a drink and talking about the day. Jono was thrilled at the pictures Maxwell took. "I really look like a surfer!" she exclaimed. "You are a surfer," Maxwell confidently told her. "What do you think of this one?"

Maxwell scrolled the camera's wheel to a photo of Jono being carried out of the water by Mike. "Oh man… this is good. Please send this one to me right away," she pleaded. Jono was still on a high from the whole experience. Maxwell saw Mike approaching while Jono was still engrossed in the pictures. He tapped Jono on the shoulder and she looked up at Maxwell, then looked to see what he was looking at. "Holy shit!" Jono burst out. Mike slowly approached them, with no emotion on his face; the only thing on his face was a small piece of tissue with a dab of blood on it. The beard was gone! Jono and Maxwell both stood. Jono's mouth was hanging open; Maxwell reached over and closed it. Jono embarrassingly smiled. Mike looked so different without the nasty black beard, much younger. His face was chiseled, he had high, strong cheekbones, a narrow chin, and his lips were *perfect*, Jono thought to herself. "What'd you do with our friend Mike?" Maxwell joked. Mike smiled.

"I hope you don't mind, I saw the razor there and couldn't resist," he told them, shrugging his shoulders. He was still wearing the nasty clothes he'd been wearing since the first day they met him. "Hold on," Jono told him as she slowly walked past him, staring at his face. "Remarkable," she pronounced. Then darted off across to the house. "Where's she going?" Mike asked Maxwell; Maxwell shrugged his shoulders. Seconds later, Jono reappeared with a large shopping bag in her hands. Maxwell smiled. She handed the bag to Mike. "What's this?" he asked.

Jono smiled coyly. "I hope you don't mind, but your clothes have seriously seen better days." Mike held up the bag. "I don't think I can except these," he started to say. "If you want to eat dinner with us you can," Jono told him, waving her finger at him. Maxwell thought it was funny; Mike didn't change his expression. Mike wasn't sure what to do. "Look, I couldn't help it, I had to: no offense, really. If you don't like the clothes or you don't want them, then after dinner just give them back. No big deal. I didn't even pick them out, Maxwell did - with my approval, of course."

"Of course," Maxwell added. Kale came out on the deck. "Dinner's ready," he announced. "Oh great, I'm starved." Maxwell got up and walked inside the house. "This way, Maxwell," Kale told him, pointing toward the beach. "It's such a beautiful night, the missus and I thought you might enjoy having dinner on the beach."

"That is great," Jono said to Kale.

"Works for me!" Maxwell added as he headed toward the Tiki lights he could see on the beach. Mike just stood there, holding the bag.

"Well, what are you waiting for? Go change, let's eat," Jono strongly suggested. Mike didn't say a word and walked back into the house. "How beautiful is this?" Jono asked Maxwell. "Amazing," he expressed. "How are you doing?" Maxwell leaned in closer to Jono and took her hand. Jono looked at him.

"Are you okay?" she sarcastically asked him.

"Exactly. That's what I want to know… are *you* okay?" Maxwell sincerely asked her. Jono knew he was being serious so she answered seriously. She smiled at him.

"You're going to think I'm nuts or have lost my mind or something," she started. "These last few days… I just feel so different," she tried to convey to him. Maxwell listened intently. "I'm not sure how to explain it, but it's real, I like this feeling. I don't know." She took a long pause. "Maybe it's the I-almost-died thing, or maybe I got some island fever that's making me this way. Like I said, I'm sure you think I've lost my mind."

"Or… if I may, you're happy?" Maxwell squeezed her hand. Just then Mike approached. "I'm sorry."

"Nope, it's good," Maxwell told him. "Please have a sit. I took the liberty of picking some wine for us, I hope that's okay?" Maxwell asked their guest. "I'm not much of a drinker, so I trust your judgement."

"Did you hear that?" Maxwell said, looking at Jono.

"Mike, the clothes look great on you. I hope you like them." Mike was nodding his head. "I do. I'm amazed that you got my sizes right," he added.

"Oh, all that credit goes to Maxwell. He's kind of an expert when it comes to judging sizes," she explained. The dinner's first course showed up. "Amazing," Jono told Kale. Kale nodded in appreciation.

"So, Mike... Jono and I were just talking, and we realized we know almost nothing about you. I mean, we know you were a fireman, thank God, and you came to Hawaii for vacation and stayed... but really not much more. Do you mind sharing a little?" Maxwell asked. Jono didn't want to gang up on Mike or make him uncomfortable so she stayed out of it. She was happy Maxwell asked the questions, though. Mike nodded his head, then took a rather large gulp of his wine. "I guess so. Not much to tell, really. Where would you like me to start?" he asked, looking at Jono.

"It doesn't matter, anywhere you want," Maxwell answered. "How old are you?" Maxwell blurted out. Jono gave him a dirty look. Mike laughed.

"I must look much older than I am," Mike chuckled.

"Not anymore," Jono smiled.

"I'm twenty-nine. Just turned twenty-nine, actually."

"Well, Happy Birthday!" Maxwell told him. "We'll have to have Kaleen make us a special dessert!" he added.

"Happy Birthday, Mike," Jono told him.

"Thanks, guys. Yup, so I grew up in Southern California, just a few miles from the beach, hence the surfing. I became a fireman right after I graduated college, moved to Denver, then got married at twenty-three to the love of my life. She and I had one child, a beautiful daughter named Macie."

Jono was literally scared to say or ask anything more. She gave Maxwell the eye, like 'that's enough'.

"Unfortunately I lost both of them two and a half years ago from a terrible boating accident here in Hawaii." Mike took another big swig of his wine. Jono wanted to stop him, but it was as if he needed to tell them. "The guy who killed my family was some low-level Saudi prince, and he was never prosecuted. I heard he went home and has never set foot in the United States since."

"Wow," Jono said very quietly.

"After that… I gave up. I quit. I had no reason to keep living. I wanted nothing, I wanted no one, I didn't want to live." His eyes were bloodshot red, full of water. He reached up and wiped them with his napkin before a tear could fall. "I tried…" He looked at Jono and Maxwell. "…but I couldn't do it. I kept seeing my baby's face. She wouldn't want me to end my life, she wouldn't want to be responsible, so I didn't." Mike took a long pause and a deep breath. "I've been walking the beaches, surviving off the land ever since."

Neither Jono nor Maxwell said a word. They couldn't: how do you respond to such a tragic personal story? Jono wiped away a tear of her own. "But look! Now you're here, living in this amazing place, giving surfing lessons! What more could a man ask for?" She reached out and took Mike's hand. "You are an amazing person. Thank you for sharing that." Jono's heart was pounding out of her chest. She smiled as best she could.

"Yes. Thank you," Maxwell told him, wiping the water from his eyes. "And on a lighter note, here comes dinner!" Maxwell announced. Kaleen and Kale brought out trays of food: sea bass was the main course. They ate and drank, talked and laughed. Great stories, funny stories, but most of the conversation was about Jono's surfing prowess. Mike the loner, the former fireman who had been in dire pain for over two years, changed in the course of that dinner. The pain was drifting away: he was more relaxed, more open, smiling. "So," Mike interrupted the flow. "I actually don't know you guys at all either. Time for your story, don't you think?" Mike smiled.

"Sure, I guess so," Jono said. She was relieved that he finally asked: she would have felt awkward just telling him who she was.

"So I would have guessed this was your house until I saw the inside," Mike told them. *A curious remark*, Maxwell thought.

"How do you mean? I mean you're right, it's not my house, but why don't you think so?" she inquired, also intrigued by the comment.

"It's got 'rich male' written all over it, I'd assume unmarried."

"Wow, that's good," Maxwell told him. "The house belongs to a friend of ours, he's letting us use it for a while."

"So where are you guys from?"

"Los Angeles. Both of us," Jono answered.

"Really? LA, that kind of makes sense. You said Maxwell is your manager or something like that, didn't you?" Jono nodded. "So you must be an actress or a model maybe?" Mike smiled.

Maxwell sat there quietly, trying hard not to laugh. "Yes, I'm a model." Jono almost felt guilty answering the question. She was surprised her name alone didn't set off any bells for Mike, but the truth was that she was happy for the anonymity, something Jono never got.

"Ah, a model. That explains a lot," he told them.

"Explains what?" Jono felt like she was about to be offended.

"You're perfect. Everything about you is perfect. You are so beautiful, you could only be a model." Jono was shining inside; she wanted to leap across the table and kiss him.

"Yeah, beautiful. Since you've met me, not so much. I've been either blue from dying or covered in sand and water. A wreck, I think. Zero make-up, hair everywhere," she laughed as she punched Maxwell in the arm. "Ouch!"

"The truest sign of beauty, natural beauty," Mike said sincerely.

"Man! You're saying all the right things, that's for sure!" Maxwell laughed. Jono socked him again. Maxwell moved his chair closer to Mike, out of reach of Jono. "You've never heard of Jono before?" Maxwell asked, hesitantly surprised.

Mike shook his head. "No. I'm sorry, that's bad, isn't it?" he asked Jono. This time Jono was shaking her head.

"Bad? Noooo, that's good," she smiled.

"I don't think I've watched television in ten years. I have no idea I last looked at a magazine. You are obviously very successful, you must be," he suggested.

"What makes you say that?" Maxwell asked.

"Well, besides having friends in high places," he nodded toward the house, "you seem to be a one-name person, you know, like Madonna and Izy." Jono burst out laughing. She laughed so hard she nearly fell to the sand. Maxwell and Mike laughed along. Maxwell was really looking forward to see how Jono was going to handle this question. Jono calmed down then cleared her throat; she took a drink of her wine.

"Hum. Sorry, that was just so funny. I guess you're right, though, I am or have become one of those *one*-name people. Oh man, that's just so funny." Jono was starting to lose it again, but quickly snapped out of it. "My name Jono means nothing, comes from nowhere, it has no purpose. The sad truth is my dad, whom I've never known, got my alcoholic mother pregnant. She decided to have me, for what reason I don't know, except I'm convinced she was looking for child support, and I know sadly she was getting money from the government for being a single mom. So… what happened is… the jerk he is, my sperm donor dad showed up at the hospital the day I was born. My mom, she says, was asleep when a nurse came into her room and asked my dad to fill out some paperwork, which included naming me. My mom says he put 'Jon' after himself: truth is, I think he put 'Jon' where he was supposed to put his name. Who knows? He left, never to be seen or heard from again. Apparently, the next day the nurse came back into my mom's room and questioned the name, wondering if it was a mistake. My mom…" Jono took a deep breath, "the only thing my mom could think of was to add the 'o', and told the nurse my name wasn't Jon, but Jono. Pathetic really. Anyway, that's the story. By the time I was old enough to do anything about it, I was stuck with it. Of course, after Maxwell and I got together, he wouldn't let me change it anyway: he loved it." Jono smirked at Maxwell.

"Wow, that is a story. Not one I'll soon forget!" Mike smiled.

"And not one you can tell," Maxwell strongly explained.

"Oh. Sure, of course. Your secret is safe. Unless of course someone offers me a lot of money!" He smiled coyly. Jono laughed; Maxwell didn't.

"So, if you don't mind me asking, what happened that first night I met you?" Mike asked, referring to the near drowning: a question Jono knew had to come up, but was hoping it wouldn't.

"I think this is where I step out," Maxwell announced as he got up from his chair.

"Oh I'm sorry, I..." Maxwell interrupted him. "It's nothing, I need to return some emails and get to bed early. You guys have a nice evening and I'll catch up with you later." He walked over to Jono and kissed her on her head. Not too late, you," he smiled. "Mike, it was truly a pleasure." He reached out to shake Mike's hand. Mike stood and shook his hand. "Likewise." With that, Maxwell disappeared back into the house.

"I feel bad, maybe I shouldn't have asked any more questions?"

"No, it's nothing like that, really. Maxwell is my oldest and only friend, he knows every aspect of my life. I'm sure he didn't need to hear it again," Jono joked.

"Oh." Mike looked at Jono. Even in the dim light of the Tiki torches she was stunning. So beautiful. *Heads must turn everywhere she goes,* he thought. He had no idea whom he pulled out of the water that night, and he didn't care. Now that he'd gotten to know Jono a little, he wanted to learn more. Jono looked at Mike; neither said anything. Mike felt a little uncomfortable, so he reached for the wine and filled their glasses.

"The truth is," Jono started. "I had an ultra-shitty childhood; I was discovered by Maxwell at thirty; thanks to him, I am, I guess, considered one of the top models in the world and I'm super-rich," she joked. Jono wasn't sure why but she didn't feel comfortable telling Mike this.

Mike sat back in his chair and took a drink of his wine. "This is why you tried to kill yourself?" Jono realized Mike knew little of her story, who she really was, why she was in Hawaii and, least of all, what happened that night.

"No. I didn't *try* to kill myself, at least not consciously anyway. I was drunk out of my mind: truth is, I don't remember a thing about that night. I don't remember being at this amazing house, I don't remember going in the water, and I definitely don't remember you!" she admitted.

Mike smiled. "Well, I remember you." Jono smiled back. She went on to tell Mike a great deal about herself, her life and the circumstances that led to that night. When she spoke about Troy you could see Mike's face tighten up. He didn't even know the guy but already didn't like him.

"So, that's the gist of it. Pathetic little girl with mommy issues, with too much money and fame. I live every woman's dream, but I feel like crap. I actually hate my life."

"You're right."

"I am? About which part?"

"That's pathetic!" Mike laughed. Jono reached over and smacked him on the arm.

"Yeah, I know, stupid. Just telling you my story makes me feel like a selfish idiot."

"So why don't you do something else, or just quit?" Mike asked sincerely. "I mean if it makes you that miserable."

"I can't quit or do something else. Trust me, I've thought about it. Too many people rely on me, especially Maxwell. He saved my life... Hey... just like you did!" she smiled. "Besides, the public would never let me," she told him.

"Public? What does that mean?" Mike thought that was a strange comment.

"It's really hard to explain. Impossible really, until you experience it for yourself. The public won't leave you alone, not when your face is on so many magazines all over the world. There is nowhere I can go, nowhere I can hide. Someone will always be looking for me, trying to get one more picture, one more sensational story: everyone wants a piece of me." Jono was getting frustrated just explaining it.

Mike reached over and took Jono's hand, and he looked her in the eyes. "I don't want a piece of you," he smiled. Jono leaped out of her chair, tackling Mike to the sand. They wrestled around, with Jono trying to find a ticklish spot - she found one and worked it hard. Mike was laughing and squirming in the sand, out of control. "Give! I give!" he yelled. Jono smiled with devious satisfaction, then sat up. In an instant Mike spun her over and now he was on top of Jono. "Not fair!" Jono screamed as she laughed. He trapped her arms, then squeezed her legs together with his feet; she couldn't move. "Slick!" Jono smiled. "Now what?" Mike hadn't even touched her yet but she was already laughing. Mike teased with his index finger. "Are you ticklish?" he asked, slowly moving his finger around her body. "No I am not!" "Really?" He hovered his finger over her ribcage. "Not here?" He drove his finger, not too hard, into Jono's ribs; she screamed and started laughing uncontrollably. "Not fair! Not fair!" she screamed. Mike stopped almost as fast as he started. She was laughing so hard she looked like she was having a hard time breathing. He was concerned he might be hurting Jono, so he rolled off of her. Jono laughed.

This time she was back on top of Mike, seemingly in control, but she wasn't. No more tickling. Jono sat on top of Mike, smiling. "Who are you?" she asked. Mike didn't respond. Jono slid down Mike's body, putting her entire weight on him, faces inches away; Mike put his arms around her back and squeezed her closer. "Are you trying to save me again?" Jono asked softly. "Do you need saving?" he responded. Jono grabbed a handful of Mike's long, dark hair. "Maybe." She leaned the rest of the way in and kissed him softly. She pulled her lips away, staying as close as possible. Something strong and powerful ran through her body; her mind was racing but not as fast as her heart. Mike reached around her head and pulled her lips back to his. It was a ravenous kiss, hard, passionate, long. They rolled around on the sand connected like they were one, neither letting up. Mike hadn't kissed a woman since his wife. Jono was receiving all of that pent-up passion and more.

Finally they broke away from each other. Jono sat up. Mike took a deep breath, then he sat up. Jono looked at him and smiled. "That was a kiss!" Mike didn't say a word. Jono jumped right back on Mike, like he had no choice, which was good with him. After hours of intensely passionate and sensual lovemaking they found themselves sitting on the beach close to the outgoing waves. Neither spoke: they watched the moonlight glimmering on the glassy water. Mike reached out and picked up Jono's hand.

"Are you okay?"

She pulled his hand to her bare chest. "Yes." Mike smiled and kissed her. Then he stood up and threw his towel on the sand. "What are you doing?" she laughed.

"Going swimming!"

"Now?"

"Yeah now, this is the best time to go. Come on!" He ran bare naked into the water. Jono stood up. "Naw, I don't think so, I'm good." She smiled. Mike ran back to her. He held both of her hands. "Trust me, don't you?" Jono nodded. "You'll see, this is almost better than surfing. Let's go." Jono dropped her towel and grabbed Mike's hand; together they ran into the water, Jono screaming the whole way. She was surprised: the water wasn't cold at all. Mike dove into an oncoming wave, and Jono followed right behind.

They floated out in the calm water, holding each other's hands, looking up at the stars for what seemed like minutes but it was nearly an hour. Jono started to shiver. Mike laughed when he heard Jono's teeth chattering. "Come here." Mike pulled her close to him; when their bodies touched, Jono got the chills but not because she was cold. She could feel the heat radiating off of Mike's body. He pulled her tight to him, wiped some hair from her face, then kissed her.

A salty, hot, passionate kiss: Jono nearly forgot where she was. They both had an experience they had never had before and would never soon forget. They swam back to shore. Jono didn't want the night to be over; she invited Mike back to the house, but Mike declined. "I'm sorry, can't, I have to go," he told her. Jono didn't understand but didn't want to beg. "Surfing tomorrow?" she asked Mike as he walked away. "Sure! Six?"

"Really?" Jono asked. Mike stopped and turned back with a big grin on his face.

"Glass off!"

"Perfect!" Jono grabbed her towel and ran for the house.

UNEXPECTED PLEASURES

Maxwell was enjoying his morning coffee out on the deck while reading some of his emails. Jono quietly approached and sat down in the chair next to him. Maxwell looked up and smiled. "Looks like it might have been a good night last night." Jono hid her smile behind her cup of coffee, looking back at Maxwell. As tired as she was, her eyes were bright, her face was… different.

"You're not going to leave me hanging here, are you? I need details!" Maxwell jokingly demanded.

"I don't know, does a girl tell?" she asked sheepishly. "Well, they shouldn't but it's me and you, so yes… All the details." He smiled. Jono took a large drink of her coffee. Kaleen brought out a tray of breakfast foods and set them on the table.

"How are you this morning, Jono?"

"I'm fine, a little tired but I'm good, really good, actually."

"Awe, that's nice, he seems like a nice boy." Jono couldn't help herself: she blushed, a rare moment, to be sure. "Eat something, it will give you some strength, especially those berries. Mr. Dan grows them right here," she explained.

"Thank you very much, Kaleen. I will."

"Did you just blush?" Maxwell accused her.

Jono turned her face away. "Flush, I'm going with 'flush'. I am pretty tired, you know?"

"Okay with me. I just don't want to miss any history-making moments!" he joked. Jono smiled: she couldn't wait to talk.

"Maxwell, last night could not have been any more perfect. I hate to say it, but really… it was magical," she tried to explain.

"Magical. Honey, you know part of me wants to jump up and down for you, be excited, celebrate this *magical* night. But before anything else I'm your friend; it's my job to protect you and tell you the truth, right? We have always had a pact that we tell each other the truth and, no matter how harsh, we would not let it affect our friendship or our business relationship, meaning you can't fire me." Maxwell was half-joking.

"Wow, this must be bad."

"No, not bad, not bad at all. I would say cautionary. It's not hard for me to see you have feeling for our beach bum, right?"

Jono stuck out her tongue at him. "Maybe."

"Yeah right. So let's back up a wee bit. You have a very serious fallout with your then boyfriend, Troy," Jono spit on the sand when she heard the name. "Oh that's just ladylike, isn't it?" Maxwell scolded her.

"I know, I hate him so much and hearing his name right now makes me sick."

"Okay, whatever. You and the *Devil* have a very intense falling out - breakup, I guess."

"You guessed right."

"You do some unscheduled scuba-diving, with no scuba tanks, and would have drowned had it not been for your hero fireman, Mike. A beach bum who, thank God, truly, was in the right place at the right time and saved your life. No one knows him, or much about him. You and I scour the island looking for him, so *you* can thank him or reward him, or whatever you were thinking at the time. Which now, I guess, he's been properly rewarded." Maxwell smiled playfully. Jono coiled up to strike but held back.

"This is a long story, but I like it, keep going." Jono smiled, holding her chin in her hands, listening intently.

"It's important!"

"Yeah, I get that. Go on."

"So after several days, after looking everywhere, talking to so many people, including the police, and passing out, what, hundreds of dollars looking for leads, he just shows up? In my book that's a little odd."

"That's it?" Jono asked.

"Come on, Jono, even you have to admit it's a little too convenient, don't you think? I mean, I like Mike, I really like Mike, but I'm worried for you. I don't know where your head is right this minute, but I can see you're falling, you're going over the edge with Mike."

Jono couldn't help but laugh. "Going over the edge?" she questioned. Maxwell shrugged his shoulders. Jono poured herself another cup of coffee. She knew Maxwell had genuine concerns and he only had her best interests at heart. So, rather than lash out like she normally would, she calmly addressed his concerns.

"Okay. I'm not going to get mad. We're going to talk about this, alright?"

"That would be great." Maxwell was a little stunned, fully expecting some serious blowback.

"Yes. Everything you say is true. You're saying, without actually saying it, that this may be some kind of a play or plot. You're worried Mike might be a gold-digger or something like that." Maxwell nodded.

"You have to look at the facts," he started. "Okay yes, he saved you, but now he knows who you are... I mean, come on, the guy has nothing. Mike sat in the hospital for two or three days waiting to be moved to jail. I'm sure he watched the news, or read a paper; your *accident* was the lead story all over the world for days. He had to know it was you he saved. That's what I'm saying."

Jono smirked at Maxwell. "Did you stop to think he came to me because he heard we were looking for him?" Jono said with a little sarcasm. "I think Mike has nothing because he chooses to have nothing. I don't think it would matter to him if I had ten dollars to my name; I know, I can feel it. Meeting Mike just happened; call it fate, or luck, whatever works for you. I don't care. I believe it is what it is, it's that simple. I mean, it's not like he was hiding in the bushes at two in the morning waiting for me to try to drown myself, right?" Maxwell wasn't sure what to say so he stayed quite. "Mike saved my life; he dove into the pitch-black water when no one else was even aware I was missing, and pulled me out; and because of his experience, pure luck on my part, saved me from a sure death, or worse, being some kind of vegetable. This is the Mike we're talking about, right?"

Maxwell nodded: he felt guilty even bringing it up. "Yes."

"Max, you love me, and I know my safety is number one. I know your instinct is to warn me... but Mike's a good guy... He's a fireman, they're all good guys." She got up and walked over to hug Maxwell.

"Well, I just want to make sure you see things as clearly as you can, before you get all tied up in knots. This is just a possible theory. It's important you keep an open mind and you look at all possibilities. My job is to protect you in *all* ways, even from love," Maxwell told her sincerely.

"I understand. So we're good?" She kissed him on top of his head. Jono moved and sat down in Maxwell's lap. She laid her head on his shoulder. "But it could also just be, right?" "Yes, it could," Maxwell said supportively. Maxwell did enough damage for one day; he decided going forward he would keep these kinds of concerns to himself. But he wasn't convinced he was wrong.

Jono and Maxwell spent the day shopping together, something they love but rarely get to do. Jono's well-thought-out disguises seemed to be working: no one had looked twice at her. They decided to stop at a little cafe that was right on the beach for a light lunch and something tropical to drink. It was a warm, beautiful day. They sat at a small table right next to a wood rail that put them over the water. It was relaxing and beautiful. The waves quietly lapped against the rocks that were under them. "This is really hard to beat," Maxwell said approvingly. Jono held up her tall, tropical drink with a blue umbrella sticking out of the top. "To more times like these," she toasted. "Yes, to more times like these," Maxwell agreed.

"We should head back, don't you think?" Jono asked Maxwell.

"You got a date?" he teased.

"Well, sort of, another surfing lesson," Jono answered somberly. Maxwell didn't like her tone at all. He knew he hurt Jono by questioning Mike's intentions, and he hated himself for it.

"Jono, I agree with you, you're probably right, but we don't know. I could be so far wrong: I hope I am. I needed to talk to you about it so you would be safe and make smart choices."

Jono looked up. "I know. But no matter what happens it's been an awesome fantasy," she smiled.

"Awe, man… Let's get home. The sooner you're in the water, the happier you will be." Jono nodded in agreement. Maxwell paid the bill and thanked the manager as they walked out to the narrow street. Two feet from the front door they were mobbed by photographers and flashbulbs. Jono screamed, and Maxwell quickly wrapped his arms around her and pushed through the crowd. The crowd was yelling so many different things at one time that nothing was discernible. The paparazzi were on a feverish rampage trying to get as close to Jono as possible. Maxwell was trying his best to push them back. So many flashes going off all at once was blinding; Maxwell was having a tough time navigating his way back to the car.

The restaurant manager followed behind, and when they made it to the car the manager blocked the door so Jono could get in. Then he did the same for Maxwell. Jono hid her head in her lap, holding her hands over her head: she didn't want to see anyone or hear any of it. It was like the previous couple of weeks had never existed; it was a beautiful dream taken away in seconds. "How did they find me, Max?" Jono asked after they got a fair distance away. "I don't know." But he had his suspicions. Maxwell knew better than to drive straight back to the house, so he gave the few cars that were following a lengthy diversion, including pulling up to the valet at three or four different resorts. After about an hour of this craziness they pulled into the guard-gated private community where Dan's house was.

Jono and Maxwell didn't talk much during the hour-long pa-parazzi getaway; Jono just thought. She was confused and hurt. She knew what Maxwell was thinking. She refused to except it, not yet. But she had to know, she had to know the truth. *Could this have been Mike?* she questioned. She didn't want to believe it. Mike was so real, the most real person Jono had ever known. If he was, in the end, only an opportunist, it would crush Jono and she would be scared forever.

Jono went to her room to rest; Maxwell grabbed a drink and went out on the deck to deal with some business items and hire some additional security. Jono was out cold the rest of the day; even Maxwell dozed off in an oversized chaise lounge on the deck. It was nearly dark out. "Excuse me," a man's voice called out. "Excuse me, Maxwell," he called out a little louder, this time waking Maxwell up. Maxwell sat up. "Yes," he replied, looking around his immediate area. "I'm down here," Mike told him. Maxwell got up and walked to the deck railing. "Mike? What are you doing?" Maxwell asked, still dazed. "Oh well, I thought I was meeting Jono to go surfing, but she wasn't on the beach, I just wanted to make sure everything is alright," he said with a serious face.

"Mike, come on up here," Maxwell gestured toward the steps. Mike set down the two surfboards he brought with him, then trotted up the steps. "Have a seat. We need to talk." Maxwell was setting the tone. Within a minute Kaleen had a pitcher of her ice tea and some snacks on the table. "Thank you, Kaleen." Maxwell smiled at her.

"What's wrong, Maxwell? Is Jono alright?" he asked as he slid his chair in closer to the table. Maxwell poured them both a glass of tea. "Jono had a rough day today," he started. "Somehow someone discovered she's here in Hawaii and found us at a small cafe in town. Jono was devastated. Her peace was broken."

"Oh man. I feel so bad for her. I can't believe it, things were fine. What happened?" Mike was actually starting to get visibly upset. Maxwell was happy to see this reaction.

"Honestly, Mike, I have no idea. I know it wasn't Kaleen or Kale, they just wouldn't do that: they're paid very well not to do that. Beside myself and you, no one else knows she's here." Mike was shaking his head, he was getting pissed off. How was this going to affect his time with Jono? Would they still be able to be... well, friends?

"Mike, I have no choice, I have to ask you and, more importantly, you have to be honest with me," Maxwell said in a very serious tone.

"You want to know if I told anyone?" he asked before Maxwell did. Maxwell nodded his head. "No, I've spoken to no one. I don't ever speak with anyone, not until I met you guys, anyway. Why would I ruin one of the best things that has ever happened to me, even if it only lasts a week, knowing Jono has changed my life." Maxwell knew he was telling the truth.

"And you hers," Maxwell confided. Mike mustered up a smile.

"I don't know who did this, but I can find out," Mike abruptly stood.

"Mike, sit down. I'm sure Jono's going to want to see you when she wakes up. Come on, have a little food." Maxwell was insisting. Mike's face was flexing with anger.

"Can I leave my boards here?" he asked Maxwell.

"Of course. But don't you want to see Jono? I know she's going to want to see you. Besides what can you really do? It doesn't matter anymore, the cat's out of the bag, and trust me once the cat is out, you ain't never getting it back in!" Maxwell was speaking from experience.

"Jono might think it was me. I need to prove to her it wasn't. I need to show her I would never do anything to hurt her," Mike declared. Whatever it was he thought he could do, he was off to do it.

"What do you want me to tell Jono?" Maxwell yelled out.

"Six in the morning tomorrow!"

"Awe, man, what's with these surfers and six in the morning?!" Maxwell thought out loud. "Crazy."

A couple of hours later, Jono emerged from her bedroom. She lazily walked out on the deck where Maxwell was eating dinner and working on his computer. "Hey, you," Maxwell smiled. Jono plopped down in the chair opposite him.

"Hey yourself. How long was I out?" she asked.

"Can't say for sure, but at least three hours."

"Really? I guess I needed it."

"I think so. How are you feeling?" Maxwell asked.

"I'm okay… a little confused and a lot upset," she admitted.

"I completely understand. You must be hungry?"

"Famished!" Maxwell didn't even have to get out of his chair: out came Kaleen with food for Jono. Jono smiled at Kaleen. "You're amazing." Kaleen nodded. "Hey, what are those?" Jono asked about the two surfboards leaning against the wall behind Maxwell.

"Ah well, those are Mike's," he tried to say light-heartedly.

"Mike's? Oh shit! We were supposed to meet at sunset to surf today! Damn. Why didn't you wake me up?" she asked sternly.

"Jono, I would have, honestly… but you were so beat-up after that incident this afternoon, I felt you needed to rest. Besides, it gave me a really good chance to talk to Mike," he told her.

"Talk to Mike? You mean drill Mike, don't you?"

"No, actually we had a short but good talk. I am one hundred percent sure it wasn't him."

"I know it wasn't him! You're the one who thought it was him!" Jono said angrily.

"Jono, I didn't say it was him, I said we had to rule out that possibility, that's all."

"So where is he? Why isn't he here?"

"Uh, he got pretty mad when I told him about someone ratting you out, and when I told him about today at the cafe, he got superpissed. He said he needed to find out who it was that told the media you are here. Then he took off."

Jono threw down her fork. "I can't eat."

"Awe come on, Jono, you need to eat, *it's your favorite*," Maxwell teased like he was talking to a child. Jono laughed, then threw her spoon at Maxwell.

"I hate you right now!" she said smiling. "Now give me my spoon back, I need it."

"So I'm clear, Mike's good, he's not upset at me, or you; you're okay with Mike and I am okay with both of you. Does that sum things up?"

"It does. Except you missed the icing on the cake… The world knows you're here." He smiled.

Maxwell went on to tell Jono all the details of the conversation he had with Mike. "What's he think he's going to do?" Jono asked.

"I'm not sure, but he looked determined." Maxwell took a very long pause, picked up Jono's hand, and leaned in as close as he could. "What?" Jono asked with a mouth full of fish. "We have another little problem," he expressed. "We do? Is it a job thing? What is it?" Jono was being snippety: whatever it was she didn't care, she just wanted Mike back. Maxwell squeezed her hand. Jono stopped eating and set down her fork. She looked right at Maxwell. "What is it, Max? What's bugging you?"

Maxwell took a deep breath. "He loves you." Jono leaned back in her chair. "He does?" she asked with a half-smile on her face. "Did he tell you that? Why would he tell *you?*" she questioned.

"No, he didn't tell me… but I know. And this is not some puppy love, fantasy, I'm-in-love-with-a-model thing, he's in deep. Kill for you deep," Maxwell emphasized.

Jono sat straight up in her chair, smiling, looking like she was thinking about it. "Okay, let's say you're right. Why is this a problem?"

"Well, let's play this out a bit. I know you like Mike a lot, a lot a lot." Jono nodded her head. "If this relationship was only going to last for the next week or two, until we *had* to leave, then I think it would sting for you, and hurt for Mike; but over time all will heal."

"Is that what you think this is? Some kind of a fling?" Jono asked sharply.

"No I don't. Mike loves you. He wants to be with you, he wants to protect you; he's a beach bum, he loves it here and he loves living off the land; he'll never leave and you can't stay." Maxwell threw the back of his hand onto his forehead. "Oh whoaies me! The drama of it all!" he jested. "This is like one of the famous love stories, like Romeo and Juliet!" He smiled. Jono sat there watching his crazy production.

"Are you back on drugs again?" she teased, shaking her spoon at him. Maxwell laughed.

"Oh, by the way, you're supposed to meet Romeo on the beach at six in the morning tomorrow," he smiled.

"Six in the morning again? What's with these surfers?" she laughed. But there was no way she was going to miss her lesson. She needed to see Mike: she had to know he was okay.

Jono and Maxwell retired to the family room to relax and catch up on some news. From the minute the television was turned on, Jono was the story.

'*Supermodel Jono was apparently spotted in Waikiki earlier today coming out of Bananas with her manager Maxwell Bean. It turns out after Jono's near life experience some weeks back here in Hawaii, she never actually left*'.

"Wow! That didn't take long," Jono said sarcastically. Maxwell changed the station several times but they were all carrying the Jono sighting story. They knew she was on the island: they weren't sure where and they didn't know for how long. Jono and Maxwell knew that, even if they never left the house, it was only a matter of time until she would be discovered. Either way it didn't really matter. Jono needed to be in LA for fitting as soon as possible: since she had a major shoot in Milan in two weeks' time.

"We have to go," Maxwell told her.

"I know."

"It needs to be yesterday."

"I know. Make the arrangements, but give me at least a couple more days."

"Yup, no problem. What are you going to do about Mike? You're going to have to break it off. He'll just have to understand," Maxwell explained. Jono turned off the television.

"Do I?" she questioned.

"What do you mean?" Maxwell asked. Jono gave Maxwell the look. "Awe, man. What are you thinking now?" he asked, not sure if he really wanted the answer.

"I'm going to invite Mike to come to LA and hang out. If he wants, he can come to Milan with us. He'd love it!" She started to get excited.

"He'll say no."

"Really? You think?"

"I do. Why would you want to do this anyway? Is this really about Mike... or you? I don't think this is your best idea. I know you think you know him, but do you? Yes, he loves you and yes he's gorgeous, but is he... you know, stable?"

Jono laughed. "Any less stable than me?"

"That's true. Although not exactly what I was going for." Maxwell forced a smile. He knew he wasn't going to win, no matter how sound his opinion. "Fine, I guess. I'm just warning you this is going to be a mess. Don't come crying to me when he has a meltdown or you do!" Maxwell said sternly.

"First of all, if he or I have a meltdown, I'm *only* coming to you. Second, come on, think about it, if he is miserable or I am, all we have to do is put him on a plane and, poof, six hours later he's back home roaming the beaches in Hawaii. But honestly, I don't see that."

"Okay then. Good luck." Maxwell said his goodnights and disappeared down the hall. Jono sat there for a few more minutes thinking about Mike and wondering if he would come with her. *How do I even ask him?* she pondered. She couldn't stop thinking about him, his life, what he'd been through. How much she cared for him. *Is this possible?* she asked herself. *I've known him for four days, what the heck? Maybe Maxwell's right. Maybe this is one of those Nightingale things. Crap.*

At ten minutes to six, Jono's alarm went off. She sprang out of bed, threw on her surfing attire, grabbed her robe and headed for the kitchen. Kaleen was already there waiting with a container of coffee and two mugs. "Wow. Kaleen, you are truly amazing. How did you know?" Jono asked, sipping on her coffee. Kaleen smiled. "Just a feeling."

"Man, I wish I could do that. I'm taking a gamble right now on *just a feeling*." Jono smiled. "Most of the time my *just a feelings* don't work out so well," she jokingly admitted.

"You're speaking of Mike?" Kaleen asked.

"Yeah I am."

"You care about him. I can tell."

"I do. Kind of scary how much, actually." Jono half-smiled.

"There's a Hawaiian saying, which is old and too long..." Kaleen laughed at herself. "Basically it says, *don't think with your head, feel with your heart. Your heart will never lie to you.*"

"Uh... wow. I like that. It makes a lot of sense, doesn't it?"

"It worked for me," Kaleen told her. "Listen, child, I know it's not my place to say anything, but you need to know: Mike has been broken like few ever are. I don't think he could be broken again," she said somberly. Jono stood there for a second thinking about what Kaleen just told her.

"I know. I would never do that, I couldn't do that."

"Trust your heart, everything will be fine."

Jono grabbed the coffee and the mugs and headed out the door. "Thank you, Kaleen!"

Mike was wading in the water when Jono came running up. "You're late!" he joked as he met her on the beach.

"I know, I'm sorry, I was getting us some coffee: here." She poured him a cup.

"Perfect, thank you." He leaned in and kissed her, catching Jono off guard. "Oh, I'm sorry." Mike was immediately embarrassed.

"No no. Sorry. My mind was somewhere else, that's all." With that Jono leaped onto Mike, wrapped her legs around his waist, and held onto him around his neck, kissing him passionately. "Is that better?" she teased.

"Better," he smiled. He set her down. "So are we doing this or what?"

"I'm ready," she told him. Mike walked over to the two surfboards he had lying on the beach: one was the longboard they'd been using, the other was much shorter with crazy graphics and scary-looking fins on it. Mike picked up the longboard and headed for the water. "What's with this other board?" Jono asked him. "That's for later!" he yelled back. "Oh." Jono ran to catch up. A perfect day, with awesome medium-sized waves breaking a fair distance from the shore. Other surfers also thought it was a great day to surf: there must have been over fifty surfers in the water paddling around in the general area. "There goes the neighborhood!" Jono joked as they made it out past the breakwater.

"Yeah. Listen, Jono, we'll give this a few tries, but today might not be the best day for us to surf," he strongly suggested.

"Why?" She didn't understand. *Just because there are other surfers in the water?* she quietly questioned.

"The waves are quite a bit larger, look at the foam." Mike pointed back toward shore. Jono was fascinated to watch the other surfers from this perspective. *They are so powerful, so confident.* Then she saw one particularly hard wipe-out. "Oh my God!" she shrieked. She and Mike weren't as far out as the other surfers, but the waves were still much larger than Jono has surfed on before. Mike didn't like it and was ready to call it a day. "Are you sure you want to do this?" Mike asked again. Jono was very nervous, scared really, but she was determined at least to try.

"If anything happens, I've got you here to rescue me, right?" She leaned over to kiss Mike, nearly flipping off her board. Mike laughed.

"Okay, get ready then, looks like you've got a good one headed your way." Jono turned to see a wave starting to form behind her. She took a big gulp, then lay down on her board and started to paddle in the direction of the wave. She had to paddle a fair distance away from Mike to get into position. She turned her board and waited. Mike was swimming after her, and the wave was building. Jono lay down and got ready. Seconds later, she got a strange sense and turned her head to her right: another surfer moved in only feet away from her. Mike started yelling to Jono, telling her to let the wave go but she couldn't hear him; she paddled madly, and almost instantly the large wave had her board and was thrusting her forward. She moved her hands under her chest and without thinking leaped up to her feet.

She was up and riding the wave. At first she was a little scared: she was moving so fast and the wave was so large, but then all of Mike's training kicked in. She bent her knees, separated her feet, and held our her arms to stabilize the board. Just as she was putting it all into place, totally aware of all the sensations, no longer anyone or anything else in her mind, her surfboard was violently struck from behind by a faster-moving surfer. She and the board crashed hard at the bottom of the wave, Jono put her hands over her head to protect herself from the loose surfboard. She was thrashed about until the wave collapsed on top of her, forcing her deep into the water. Jono didn't panic; she couldn't see, so she felt around for the ocean floor, but she couldn't feel anything. She kicked as hard as she could, but, instead of taking her to the surface, she crashed head and shoulder first into the ocean bottom. She turned around and started to kick again; she was running out of breath. One more hard kick, while using her arms to try to swim out, and she finally broke the surface only to be pulled right back down by the next crashing wave. She barely had a chance to take a breath, but she knew what to do. She waited on the bottom for a few seconds then pushed again as hard as she could. This time she was above the surface in seconds. She saw the next wave coming, turned toward the beach and started swimming as hard as she could. In seconds her body was being raced toward the shore. As soon as she thought she could stand, she put down her foot and rolled in the foam of the wave. She stood up in the knee-deep water. Blood was streaming down her face. She reached up and touched the top of her head. "Ouch!" she yelped. She slowly walked out of the water toward the beach. A young man aggressively approached her just as she made it to the beach. "What the hell?" he yelled at her, holding his board in one hand, his other waving at her in anger. "These are my waves, bitch!" Before Jono could say anything, and before the young man could say another word, he was struck in the face from behind, knocking him out. There stood Mike.

"Are you alright?" He ran up to her and grabbed her face. Without saying anything else, he had a hold of her head. "Coral. We've got to get this cleaned out. Kaleen will have what we need." Mike ran and grabbed both boards, tucked them under one arm, took Jono by the hand, and walked her to the house. Mike yelled for Kaleen as they approached: both she and Kale came running out. "What's the matter?" Kaleen yelled. "Coral," Mike responded. Kaleen turned and ran right back into the house. Kale took the surfboards from Mike and directed him to take Jono to the kitchen. Jono was getting a little light-headed; her knees started to wobble, and Mike reached down and picked her up. "Here we go again," Jono smiled. Mike was very worried and upset but managed a smile. "I guess so."

Kaleen was waiting in the kitchen. "Sit her down here," she said, pointing at one of the kitchen stools. Jono laughed. "It's just a scratch, right?" Mike put pressure on the wound. It was a pretty good-sized gash, but not deep. Kaleen first rinsed the wound with some fluid then padded it with some gauze. She moved Jono's hair so she could see the wound better, then gently wiped some bits of coral out of the cut. "Ow!" Jono yelped loudly. Kaleen rinsed again. "She's going to need a few stitches," she told Mike.

"Who's going to need stitches?" Maxwell asked as he entered the kitchen. Before he got the words completely out of his mouth, he saw Jono's face and shirt covered in blood, with Mike holding something on her head. Maxwell nearly fainted: he and blood didn't work. He kept it together and walked right up to Jono and Mike. "What the hell did you do this time?" Maxwell scolded her. He was serious. Jono smiled. Mike tried to explain, but Maxwell didn't have the patience to listen. "I'll get the car." He quickly ran out the front door. Mike picked up Jono, and she smiled. "What would I do without you?"

"Kaleen, would you mind coming with us?" Mike asked her. "No, of course not, just let me get my bag." Mike carried Jono out to the car and with Maxwell's help put her in the back seat. Kaleen jumped in the back with Jono. As they pulled out of the gated community, Maxwell hung up his cellphone. "Okay, they're expecting us. Someone will meet us in the back," he announced to everyone in the car. Jono was starting to feel the pain. "I guess I'm not ready for the big time!" she laughed, but was directing the comment at Mike. "Yeah, I guess not," Maxwell jumped in angrily. The rest of the ride to the small local hospital was oddly quiet.

Jono was whisked away in a wheelchair with the others in tow. The nurse took them into a small office. "What are we doing in here?" Maxwell snapped at her. "There is nowhere else in the hospital that is private," she explained. "Oh." Mike sat in a chair next to Jono. "You're going to be fine, it's a small cut," he told her. Jono leaned over and kissed him. "Mike, can I speak to you outside for a minute?" Maxwell asked in a low stern tone. Jono was going to intervene, but just then the nurse came back into the office with a doctor. "It might be a good idea to have everyone step out for a few minutes," the nurse instructed. She invited Kaleen to stay behind, which she gladly did. Mike and Maxwell walked outside to the back of the hospital.

Mike barely cleared the door when Maxwell jumped hard into Mike. "Mike, Mike. Who are you?" he asked with a really intense voice. Mike stood there looking at Maxwell, stunned but listening. He didn't try to answer. "Look, Jono thinks she knows you, and maybe she does, but I know you know her!" Mike wanted to say something but, out of respect for Jono, he didn't. "Jono is a supermodel, a SUPER model: you know what that means, don't you? She is known and loved all over the world; people pay her crazy amounts of money to wear and model their clothes. Everyone who is anyone wants a piece of Jono. And today... you nearly let her get killed!" Maxwell was getting more pissed as he talked. This time Mike had to say something.

"You know I would never hurt Jono, I would give my life to protect her. I know some things changed. You don't trust me for some reason, maybe you think I'm loony or something, which I could understand, but I'm not. It's true, for a number of years I lived in a fog, but not anymore, for the first time in a long time my mind is clear, that's because of Jono. I know you don't really know me... and I can't ask you to trust me, but maybe you can give me a chance. That's all I want: a chance."

Maxwell sat down on top of a small retaining wall and put his face in his hands. Mike sat down next to him. "I know you think you love her, and that's great. Really. But have you thought past today?" He lifted his head and looked Mike directly in the eyes. Mike didn't speak. "Mike, have you thought about how things would be or could be past today or tomorrow?" Maxwell pressed. "Jono can't stay here in Hawaii, you must know that; she has a life, responsibilities, contracts! Shit, Mike! Have you thought about any of this?" Maxwell was being direct and mean, but everything he was saying was true. Mike hadn't allowed himself to think past today: he couldn't. Mike's head hung down low. Maxwell put his hand on his shoulder.

"Listen, Jono and I are leaving tomorrow, we have to; Jono has a big job coming up." Mike stood up: his reality was taking hold. "But..." Mike started to ask. He had a heaviness in his eyes.

"I know. I also know Jono likes you - she likes you a lot. But you really need to understand: Jono's life, her real life, not this vacation, is crazy. Her life doesn't allow time for a meaningful relationship; she can't just drop what she's doing and dart off to Hawaii to go surfing when the mood hits her. That's not her reality right now. You understand?" Mike reluctantly nodded. "You want what's best for her, don't you?"

"Of course."

"You agree Jono staying in Hawaii or you going with her is not a good idea right now, right?" Maxwell pressed.

"Go with her?" That threw Mike off.

"Yes, go with her. Jono was or is going to ask you to come with us to Los Angeles."

"Really. When?"

"Today, I guess."

Mike looked desperately confused. "And you don't want me to go, is that it?"

"No... Well, yes. I don't think it's a good idea... at least right now."

"Huh. And if I'm understanding you correctly, you also don't think I'm good for Jono, or her career... right now. Is that right, too?" Mike was getting angry: his voice was deeper, his questions more direct. "Seems to me Jono is pretty happy when we're together. How is that a bad thing for her or her career?" Mike asked sharply.

"Mike, look. I'm trying to reason with you. I'm trying to be nice, but you're not making it too easy."

"What are you talking about?" Mike's body physically changed; he was getting red, his muscles tightened. Maxwell took a breath and held up his hand at Mike.

"Hold on, calm down. We're just talking. I know you don't believe me, but I'm trying to help you. I'm trying to explain to you that's it's not you; even if she wanted to, Jono doesn't have time for you... or anybody. And you... well, come on. For the last two and a half years you have been doing nothing. Just hanging out on the beach, all the time in the world with no cares. Trust me, you couldn't keep up with Jono and her needs, and she won't be able to slow down for you. It's just reality. You guys, whatever that means, won't make it. Sure, maybe for a few days, maybe weeks, but when Jono really kicks into gear, it's like being with a rockstar, she has a 24/7 life."

Mike sat back down on the wall next to Maxwell. He looked at Maxwell as if to say he understood.

"Mike, right now you are living your life on your terms. The minute you step into Jono's life that will change one hundred percent. Are you ready to have your photograph taken thousands of times a day?" Mike shook his head. "Are you ready for reporters to pound you everywhere you go? Asking you personal and uncomfortable questions?" Mike shook his head. "And how are you going to handle it when they find out about your wife and daughter..." Maxwell was abruptly interrupted.

"What are you talking about? Why would that ever come up?"

"These people are relentless. They'll dig into everything, every part of your life."

"But why, I'm nothing," he questioned.

"The minute you're seen with Jono, you become something. That's how it works. You'll have to be prepared to handle it."

The talking stopped, and they both sat there. Maxwell actually felt bad for Mike. He could see Mike's head racing with thoughts, spinning out of control. Then the silence was finally broken. "Here we are!" Jono announced happily as she was being pushed out of the hospital in a wheelchair, with the whole top of her head wrapped in white gauze. Mike ran to Jono and kissed and hugged her. He held her head close. "Are you okay?" he asked.

"I'm fine. What's going on? Are you okay?" she asked Mike. Maxwell stepped up and kissed Jono on the cheek.

"So what's the verdict?" he asked the nurse. The nurse explained that Jono had only needed a couple of stitches and they tried their best not to cut away any of her hair. "Her hair? Oh crap!" Maxwell burst out. "I watched the whole thing, no one will be able to see anything," Kaleen spoke up. "Oh, thank God." Maxwell looked sternly at Jono who was looking sternly back at him. "Should we go?" Kaleen asked. "Yes please," Jono requested.

Maxwell ran and got the car. The others sat in the shade waiting. Jono was holding Mike's hand tightly; every few seconds he looked down at her, and she was looking up at him. "This isn't your fault," Jono spoke up. Mike knelt down to be closer. "It is. I should have known better," he explained, holding her hand up to his face. Jono stroked his face. "You know... that's probably true... you dummy! What were you thinking?" she lashed out. Mike stood up: he was in shock. Jono had the biggest smile on her face. Mike reluctantly smiled back, and Kaleen and the nurse burst out laughing.

"Sorry, I had to get that dreary look off your face!" Jono laughed, too. Mike let out a sigh of relief, then chuckled. "If you want to be with me, you have to expect the unexpected!" Jono smiled.

"Be with you?" Mike asked.

"Ya well, I was going to talk to you about it later, but I think later is already here," she told him.

"What is it? What are you talking about?" Mike asked but knew exactly what she was talking about.

"I think..." She was stopped mid-sentence as Maxwell pulled up the car. Maxwell jumped out and opened the back door. Mike picked up Jono and, just as he was about to place her in the back seat, someone yelled out, "Hey!" Everyone turned to look, suddenly a flash went off. "Thank you!" the young man yelled out as he ran away.

"Well, that's it," Maxwell commented.

"Just get me home," Jono demanded sternly.

At first no one in the car spoke. Jono squeezed Mike's hand hard; every once in a while they would glance at each other and smile. Jono finally spoke up. "Maxwell, are all of our travel arrangements taken care of?" she asked very sweetly. "Yes, everything is set. We fly out tomorrow afternoon around two," he explained.

"How many tickets did you get?" she asked. Maxwell was completely caught off guard. He looked at Jono in the rear-view mirror. Jono's lips were pursed; she wasn't smiling.

"Uh, well, two. I wasn't aware there were any changes." They pulled into the driveway of the house. "You must be starving!" Kaleen said to Jono. "I am." "No problem, how about lunch on the deck in fifteen minutes?" she suggested. "That would be beautiful. But just for Mike and me, okay?" she told Kaleen. She gave Maxwell a stern look. "Yes, of course."

Jono and Mike sat at the table on the deck, drinking some of Kaleen's fabulous tea. They were both looking out toward the sea. "Water looks rough," Jono commented.

"Yeah, it is. Must be a storm somewhere."

"I guess no more surfing for me, at least on this trip. I'm totally bummed," she smiled at Mike. "You know I had that wave, I was in control... until that idiot ran into me."

"I know, I saw the whole thing. I'm sorry I couldn't get to you sooner," Mike said, obviously feeling bad about the whole incident.

"It was no big deal, I did get a little scared, though, when that guy threatened me on the beach. I'm glad you were there for sure." She smiled. Kaleen brought out lunch and placed it on the table. "Anything else I can get you?" she asked. "No. Thank you so much, Kaleen, for everything," Jono smiled at her. "She's amazing," Jono said to Mike. "She is. A special lady," he agreed. Jono and Mike turned their attention to the lunch.

Jono took maybe two bites of her salad: she couldn't hold back. "I can tell Maxwell said something to you about me wanting to ask you to come with me to LA. I'm really sorry about that. I had it all planned out but..." She pointed to her head. "I must look lovely," she realized with the large, white wrap on her head. In an instant she pulled it off and tossed it over the side of the deck, leaving only a small bandage covering her wound. Mike chuckled. "Anyway, I wanted to invite you to come with me to Los Angeles." Mike was already shaking his head no. Jono started to get a little upset. "Why are you shaking your head no? I haven't even finished yet." She paused. "What did Maxwell say to you exactly?" She was more direct with Mike than she had been. Mike looked at her and smiled.

"This isn't about Maxwell, this is about you," Mike started. "Jono... You turned my life around, you brought me back. You are an amazing person, I am honored for the time we've spent together, a memory that will always be right here," he told her pointing to his heart.

"Why are you doing this?" Jono was getting more upset. "Did I do something to you? You don't want to be with me, is that it?" she said angrily. "Is Maxwell really capable of controlling your life, of making decisions for you?"

"No, but he did tell me what I..."

"Ah, I see. And you didn't think it might be a good idea to talk to me before you made up your mind? Are you that weak?" Jono was shaking her head in disgust. "I'm sorry, I thought you were different, I thought... Never mind what I thought." Jono stood up and threw her napkin down on the table. Mike looked up at her: a single tear fell from her face. "I'm glad I could help. Thanks again for saving my life!" she yelled at him, then stormed into the house. Mike sat frozen. He stared at his food then pushed his plate away in anger. He wasn't confused, he was never confused; he loved Jono. He would do anything to be with her, but more, he would do anything to help her. He realized Maxwell was right: being in her life wasn't going to help her; it might even hurt her. He stood, thought about going into the house but then turned and walked off the deck toward the beach.

Jono never left her room the rest of that night or the next day. She refused to speak with Maxwell. He begged but she wouldn't respond, let alone open her door. She didn't want to see him; she didn't want to see anyone. Kaleen brought food to her room. She even tried to talk to Jono, but it wasn't going to happen. It wasn't until the limo showed up that Jono emerged from her room. Maxwell was waiting at the front door, Jono walked right past him without looking at him, without saying a word. Maxwell wanted to say something but decided against it. Kaleen and Kale were waiting out in front. Jono walked over and hugged Kale hard. "Thank you." "Aloha," he responded. She turned to Kaleen, smiled and hugged her. "You're the best," she told her. Then Jono whispered something into Kaleen's ear that no one else could hear. Kaleen nodded. Jono walked to the back of the car, Maxwell held the door for her, as Jono started to step in she looked at Maxwell. "You're in front," and got in. Maxwell closed the door and went and sat in the front of the limo with the driver.

In the airport and on the six-hour flight back to Los Angeles, Jono didn't say a word to Maxwell. Maxwell thought his head was going to explode. He tried to work; he watched a movie but couldn't take the silent treatment anymore. "Jono, I can't stand this anymore. Eventually you'll have to talk to me. I'm sorry. I know you think I did something wrong, but I was only looking out for you, and for Mike. It would have been a disaster." He was talking as fast as he could, but, before he could utter another word, Jono turned and looked at him as sternly as Maxwell had ever seen. She held out one finger pointing at his chest.

"Just stop. Stop right now." Maxwell nodded, then turned his body away from Jono.

The second Jono and Maxwell exited the airport in Los Angeles they were mobbed by reporters and fans. Jono had her head covered and was wearing oversized sunglasses to cover her face. The reporters were screaming questions at her: "What happened to you in Hawaii? Why were you in the hospital a second time? Who was the guy who was helping you?" And a hundred more just like that.

Between Maxwell and airport security Jono was quickly escorted to the waiting limo. This time, Jono let Maxwell sit in the back: she knew it wouldn't look good. "Home" was the only word she spoke when she sat down in the back of the car. An hour later, Jono was comfortably alone, sitting in her bed at her Malibu house. She looked out the big picture windows that faced the ocean. She stared at the waves, watching them crash on the beach in front of her home. She quickly gave into her emotions: she broke down and started to cry, eventually crying herself to sleep.

It must have been noon when Jono was startled awake. Someone was pounding on her front door. She looked at the monitor next to her bed: it was Maxwell. He was yelling something, but Jono wouldn't answer the intercom. She watched Maxwell getting more and more animated as he got more and more upset. It actually made Jono chuckle. She knew she'd have to eventually talk to Maxwell, but she didn't have to today, so she rolled over and went back to sleep.

Mike was surfing his brains out. He must have caught twenty waves in the time Kaleen had been watching. It was nearly noon when Mike finally came out of the water. Kaleen walked across the sand to get to him. "Aloha," she greeted Mike. Mike finished wiping the water from his hair, then threw his towel down on the sand. "Aloha, Kaleen."

"That was impressive," Kaleen told him.

"You were watching?"

"Sure, from up on the deck. You're really good."

Mike laughed. "Good. I guess not good enough." He tried to smile.

"I brought you something," Kaleen told him.

"Awe, Kaleen you didn't have to do that: Jono's gone. It doesn't have to be like that anymore."

"Are we not friends?" Kaleen asked with a straight face.

Mike smiled. "Yes we are." Kaleen set the tray of snacks and tea down on the sand. "What's in the bag?" Mike inquired. A small, brown paper bag was also on the tray.

"A little something from Jono, I believe." She smiled and started walking back to the house. "Bring the tray up to the house when you are done, please!" she yelled back.

"Yes, ma'am!" Mike sat down and grabbed one of the sandwiches: he was starving. He stared at the bag for a few minutes then picked it up. It was kind of heavy. *From Jono?* he thought. He reached in and pulled out a box. The box had a brand new phone in it. No note, nothing - just the phone. Mike smiled. "Strange." He opened the box and pulled out the phone. "Cool phone." He turned it on: it took a few seconds then lit up. Right as it did, a text popped up on the screen.

"Mike, I already miss you! I am so sorry for the way things were left: I was so angry at Max. Please forgive me. I wanted to give you this phone so we can stay in touch. If you ever need me for anything please call me, my number should already be programmed into the phone. I understand if you never want to speak with me again; if you think Maxwell was right, I'll just have to deal with it. But I know Maxwell is not right. I need to know you're okay, that we're okay. Contact me when you can. Love, Jono."

Mike was smiling the whole time. He checked to see if Jono's number was in the phone: it was. He wanted to call her right away, but then thought of something else. Jono was in the middle of a late dinner with Maxwell and a few of her friends when her cellphone buzzed. She picked it up off the table and looked at it. She immediately started to smile, then laughed. "What is it?" Maxwell inquired. Jono looked up. "Just a friend," she told him. She looked back down at the phone. Mike sent her a picture of a perfect little wave glistening in the sun as it headed for shore. Under the photograph there was a caption: "I see you here." Jono smiled the rest of the dinner.

Maxwell tried to apologize, but Jono wouldn't have it. "Max, just leave it be." He reluctantly agreed. Things basically went back to normal, except for two things. Jono was in contact with Mike several times a say, sending texts and photos, and occasionally they would make time for a short phone call. Maxwell never knew that Jono maintained her relationship with Mike. In fact, Mike was never mentioned at all. Then there was Jono: she had become a different person ever since returning from Hawaii. Everyone, including Maxwell, took notice. She seemed calmer, more relaxed. She rarely lashed out; she would almost always ask 'please' and say 'thank you'. Maxwell was dying to talk to her about it, but also wanted it to last as long as possible. Maxwell was always, no matter what the situation, on the receiving end of Jono being Jono. But that was Maxwell's job.

The reality of Jono's personality change really stood out on the last day of fittings before leaving for Madrid. One of the main dresses she would be working in was wrong. The hymn was wrong, the bust was wrong: someone really screwed up. Normally there would be a great deal of screaming, sometimes even random items being thrown about, then Jono often storming out of the room to go get a drink, but not this time. She looked upset, but no outburst at all. She turned to the designer. "This is not going to work," she said commandingly.

"Yes, of course you're right, this will not work," the world-renowned designer admitted. He looked terrified.

"You understand I'm on a plane tonight?" she questioned. Maxwell stood near by, unsure of what to say or do.

"Yes, yes. I know." He was waiting for it.

"No one leaves here until this is right." The designer looked up at Jono who was standing on a pedestal that designers use to work with fittings. He stood in silence for a number of seconds. "Philip, you hear me?" Jono asked sarcastically.

"Yes. I understand." He started snapping his fingers at his staff, yelling instructions in French. Everyone began to hustle around the large studio. The gown was removed from Jono, and she went and sat on the leather couch that was up against a window that overlooked downtown Los Angeles. Maxwell approached her.

"Sorry, Maxwell, that was not going to work, not even close." Maxwell was stunned.

"Yeah, I saw that. Are you okay?" he gently asked.

"No." Maxwell took a step back. "I'm starving, can you order some food? I don't care what it is, just make sure you get enough for everyone, we're going to be here a while," she politely demanded.

Maxwell was losing his mind; he felt like he was in *The Twilight Zone. Who are you and what did you do with Jono?* he dared ask only himself. "Sure. Right away." He turned to walk away.

"Oh, and Max, please find out what everyone wants to drink? I'll have some sparkling water, okay?" She smiled. He nodded and continued.

"Whoa."

Jono sat alone wrapped in a blanket on the couch, looking at her phone. Every once in a while she would burst out laughing. Everyone in the room would stop and look, then immediately go back to work. It was a surreal scene for everyone except Jono. Jono was hurriedly typing a message on her phone. "So it's settled then?" She hit 'Send'. A few seconds later, a reply: "Yes." Jono jumped up and screamed, startling everyone in the room; Maxwell nearly peed his pants.

"Are you okay?" He rushed over to her. Jono was smiling, looking nearly giddy.

"I'm good. Are we almost ready?" she asked.

Philip ran right over. "Yes, please." He directed her to the stool. This time, some three hours later, the gown was perfect. "Perfecto." Philip smiled in relief. Jono stepped off the stool. She walked over to Philip and gave him a kiss. "Yes, perfecto." She dropped the gown where she stood, threw on her jeans and tee shirt, and started walking out. "Are you coming?" She turned and looked at Maxwell. Maxwell grabbed up the rest of Jono's things and quickly followed.

Later that evening, Jono, Maxwell and Jono's staff were on a plane bound for New York: from there they would be on a red-eye to Madrid. Jono was not herself on the first leg of the flight. She was up, walking around, talking to complete strangers, unusually animated. Maxwell was worried, and tried to coax her back into her seat several times, but Jono was not interested. Maxwell gave up and went back to his computer. Then Jono came across a young, newly-wed couple who were returning from Hawaii. That was it: the empty seat next to them was occupied for the rest of the flight.

Jono was fantasied by the young couple: she wanted to know everything about who they were, where they met, and all the details about their wedding in Hawaii. The couple were at first stunned by the fact that they were talking to *Jono*, but that quickly faded and for the remainder of the flight they talked like old friends. Jono ordered champagne and had the stewardess bring the couple food from first-class. They were laughing and joking around, having a great time. The couple thought they must have been on some new show or something. The young bride asked Jono several times if there were hidden cameras somewhere.

Jono was particularly interested in the spot where the couple said their vows. "It was so beautiful," the young bride told Jono.

"It was perfect: on the beach at sunset, no one around, the waves crashing only a few feet away, it was awesome," the groom admitted. Then out came the photographs, at least the ones they had on their phones. "Fantastic!" Jono told them many times. "You are so lucky."

Several times the bride tried to ask Jono about her life, particularly her love life. "You're not married, are you?" the woman asked. Jono laughed. "No." "Isn't your boyfriend Troy Garrett?" she asked. This would have normally set Jono off: she would have stood without saying a word and walked away, but she didn't. "Troy? No. I dated him for a while, but between you and me, he was a gold-digging idiot!" She smiled. The couple weren't sure how to respond, or even if they should, so they smiled back and chuckled like they agreed.

As the plane was lining up for landing Jono asked the couple for their address. "I'd like to send you a little something, you know, as a wedding gift. It's the least I can do after you let me sit with you and take up all of your time." At first the groom resisted, but the bride started writing out the address before he could open his mouth. "Thank you. All of the best to you both. I hope your lives together are as happy as they are right now." Jono stood up to exit the plane, then turned back to the couple. "Oh, when it gets hard, or you're pissed at each other, think about this time, think about how you felt that day on the beach." She imparted her limited wisdom, smiled and walked off the plane. The young newly-weds had no idea how to respond. "Thank you!" the bride blurted out. It turned out to be a flight that would always be a great story.

For the last and longest leg of the flight, Jono put in her earplugs, put on a sleep mask, curled up with her coat and a blanket, and quickly fell asleep. She slept hard, she didn't wake until the tires of the plane screeched when they touched the runway. It was 2:00 pm in Madrid. Jono and her staff waited for the rest of the passengers to disembark the plane. Jono's hair and make-up people got busy getting Jono ready for the cameras.

Fifteen minutes later, Jono emerged from the plane with Maxwell at her side and her entourage following right behind. They were met at the gate by some of Jono's other staff, who went out early, plus her local contacts, several security guards and several uniformed police. Jono took one step out of the front of the airport and was mobbed. The clicking of cameras was almost deafening, people yelling out Jono's name. She only got a few feet from the door when she stopped. Madrid police and special security held the mob at bay. Jono smiled and struck a pose, the cameras went ballistic, and Maxwell was all smiles. She turned, and turned again, giving the cameras exactly what they wanted. Jono managed to tune out all of the questions and remarks. She waved. "I'm so excited to be here!" she told the carnivorous crowd.

She took Maxwell's arm and they worked their way to the waiting cars. As she was about to step in, one reporter yelled out above the rest, "Who's Mike?" Jono stopped and turned toward the crowd, scanning the faces. "Who's Mike?" the man asked again. Jono zoomed in on his face, smiled, then, like it was nothing, got into the car. The cars quickly drove off.

"What was that?" Maxwell asked her.

"You're asking me? I'm pretty sure this is your job!" she snapped at him. "Who was that guy?"

"I don't know."

"Well find out... please," she asked rather sarcastically. Maxwell got right on his phone. So did her personal assistant and a representative from Spain who was her local escort.

SPANISH GETAWAY

Jono and company were staying at the small but very elegant hotel Petit Palace Posada, one of the oldest hotels in Madrid. Jono was in a top-floor suite with Maxwell right next door. Before she did anything else, Jono snapped off a few photos of the view from her room and sent them to Mike. She knew he wouldn't get them till the next day: it was the middle of the night in Hawaii. Then she jumped in the shower to start getting ready for a party she needed to be at later that evening.

Jono's entourage was twenty people in total, including the escort from Spain, Michelle, two personal security guards, and two Spanish security guards. Jono didn't always like being surrounded by so many people, but in her short career she had already had too many close calls by some crazies of one sort or another, and so she embraced their presence. The party was on a huge yacht that was docked in Madrid's main marina. You could see the craft from miles away, lit up with so many lights; it was not only the largest boat Jono had ever been on, it was also the most beautiful. Lavishly decorated, brightly and meticulously polished from tip to top. The ship belonged to one of the wealthiest men in Spain, a business magnate who had his hands in just about everything, including several European fashion magazines that Jono regularly graced the covers of.

Literally hundreds of reporters, photographers and television crews were stationed behind the red velvet ropes that led to the gangway of the ship. "It looks like a small cruise ship," Maxwell said under his breath as they approached. All of Spain's fashion royalty, as well as many celebrities of all sorts, were present. When Jono's car pulled up, it was mobbed. It took several minutes before security decided it was safe for her to get out. It was only a few short steps from the car to the gangway: Jono bypassed the red carpet. She was met by her host, Fernando Del Sonata. "Greetings, my queen." He reached for her hand; Jono obliged. Fernando gave her a kiss on her hand, then a short hug. "Welcome. Everyone is excited you are here, none more than me." Jono nodded and smiled. He politely took her arm and escorted her on-board his majestic vessel.

The ship was full of the who's who not only from Spain, but also from all over Europe; Jono recognized many of them. Fernando escorted Jono onto the main deck: it was so beautiful it didn't look real. As Jono moved across the deck to a private table that Fernando had waiting for her, many reached out and shook her hand: several gave her the avant-garde two-cheek kiss, others just stared. There was no question Jono was a celebrity, but when she was in Europe she felt more like royalty. She'd never understood why, but she managed to deal with it.

Minutes after sitting down at the table with Fernando, his girlfriend, Maxwell and several other of Fernando's friends, the ship's horn blasted an ear-piercing sound announcing the ship's departure. It scared the crap out of Jono, who jumped right into Fernando's lap. Fernando and everyone else at the table laughed hard at Jono's expense. Jono let go of her heart and looked at Fernando. "Sorry," she smiled.

"It's a great day for me when a beautiful woman lands in my lap!" He laughed loudly. It was pretty funny. The ship was underway. After

Jono regained her composure, she took a big gulp of her champagne then tried to engage in conversation with her host and his friends. She was having a hard time understanding most of what was being said: the host's girlfriend didn't help much, as she didn't speak a word of English, only "Okay." Jono was getting bored quickly. She scanned the party looking for familiar faces. "Enrique!" she blurted out. Everyone turned to look, and Fernando smiled. Enrique was a Spanish movie star: young, dark, debonair.

He headed directly to the table. In Spanish he spoke with Fernando and the rest of the Spaniards for a minute or two. Maxwell and Jono smiled and politely listened. Then Enrique turned to Jono. "Hi, Jono!" He smiled. "Enrique," she nodded, trying to be somewhat cool. "Would you like to see the ship?" he asked. Jono turned and looked at Fernando. He smiled and nodded his approval. Jono was relieved. She excused herself and went with Enrique. As she walked away she looked at Maxwell and mouthed, "Sorry." Maxwell smiled and waved her on; he at least understood enough Spanish to stay in the conversation. "Wow, thank you!" Jono said to Enrique. "A little stuffy?" he laughed. "Yeah, that and I couldn't understand a word!" she joked.

Enrique must have been on this ship many times: he knew every nook and cranny. "There are no words, this is the most amazing ship I've ever seen," Jono told him.

"I know. It is really a work of art," he said. "Come on, let me show you my favorite spot." They walked to the very front of the ship, past the barriers that clearly stated, even in English, that no one was supposed to go beyond.

"Are we allowed up here?" Jono asked with a hint of concern in her voice.

"No, but that's why it's fun. Don't worry, we'll be fine," he smiled his famous smile. Jono reached out and grabbed his hand. She wasn't exactly dressed for exploring: she had to take off her shoes and pull her tight skirt up as high as she could, much to Enrique's satisfaction.

Even though they were cruising at a slow speed, within the harbor, when they stood at the very front of the ship the breeze was strong, it was breathtaking. The wind in her hair, the smell of the salt: Jono was immediately transported back to the beach in Hawaii. Enrique stood close behind her. "Beautiful, right?" he asked.

"Yes. Amazing. Thank you." She turned to face Enrique: he moved in quickly and kissed her. Jono pulled back; she had known this was coming. Standard operating procedure for Enrique, and Jono was prepared. "How many girls have you given this tour to?" Jono smiled as they started to walk back to the party.

"Oh, I don't know, one or two," he smiled.

"Uh-huh."

The party was at full speed on all decks, music blasting, people laughing, and Maxwell networking. "Hi!" Jono said, sneaking up behind Maxwell. "Oh hi," he smirked. Maxwell introduced Jono to the woman he was talking to, a fashion magazine editor whom Jono didn't know. They exchanged pleasantries. "Uh, can you excuse us, Karla? I need to speak with Jono for a minute." Maxwell took Jono's hand and walked her to a slightly quieter spot next to one of the many bars. "What's the matter?" Jono looked concerned.

"Um, well… you're not going to like it," he started. Jono hated it when Maxwell beat around the bush. She gave him the 'tell me now!' look. "Okay, okay. I wanted to warn you before you found out on your own… Troy is here," he explained. She cocked her head, and her eyes got really, really angry.

"What do you mean by *here*?" she asked, gritting her teeth.

"I mean, here, on this ship!" he said a little too loud. Jono hit Maxwell on the arm.

"Max, I don't have time for this, what are you talking about?" she demanded.

"Jono, I'm telling you five minutes ago, I exchanged pleasantries with Troy, here on-board this boat. He's here… oh and he's looking for you." Jono hit Maxwell again.

"Troy is here?" she questioned. "Do we know why he's here?"

"Yes. But you're going to hate this more." He tightened up, expecting to get hit. Jono stood there, pissed and waiting.

"Apparently, the European division for the magazine wanted Americans for the shoot. Troy was one of the guys hired." Maxwell closed his eyes.

"WHAT?!" Jono screamed. Many people turned to look, Maxwell threw up his arms, acting like this was normal. "My shoot? This can't be! *Maxwell...* how did this happen? How did *you* let this happen?" she asked in a calmer voice.

"I had no idea. I only just learned myself when he was suddenly standing in front of me. I'm just as surprised as you are."

"Yeah, but not as pissed as I am." She paused. "The shoot is in two days: you have two days to get rid of him. If they want me, they have to lose him, understand?"

"No problem. I swear, I'll take care of it." He took a deep breath. "Jono, had I known, you know..."

"I know. I'm sorry, Max. I know it's not your fault. But please take care of this?" She leaned in and kissed him on the cheek. Maxwell nodded. "Now what do I do? Trapped on a ship at sea with a rat!" She laughed. Maxwell chuckled. "I've got to find protection." She hugged Maxwell then abruptly left him standing there. "Holy crap!" he said out loud.

"Enrique!" Jono called out his name as she approached. He turned to greet her, and they exchanged a kiss. Enrique was just about to give another tour. Jono whispered in his ear: "I need your help," she requested. Enrique politely asked the young actress if he could give the tour later. She agreed and walked away. "What's the matter?" he asked. Jono went on to explain as fast as she could about Troy, their short relationship, and the fact that he was on-board the ship. And if she had to see him, she was requesting that Enrique play the role of a newfound love with her. "This I can do! I'm a great actor, you know?" "Yes, I know." Jono agreed, although she'd never actually seen a single one of his movies.

The party seemed like it was going to last all night, but thankfully a couple of hours had gone by with no sign of Troy. Jono and Enrique stayed as stationary as they could; Jono didn't want to take any chances they might run into him. "Am I a coward?" she asked Enrique. "Coward? No. I don't think so. I understand. Trust me, this kind of thing has happened to me many times. It's best to avoid confrontation, that's what I would do," he told her. Jono kissed him on the cheek. "Thank you for understanding."

"What's this?!" A voice called out. It was Troy quickly approaching. Enrique stood up from his seat. Troy got right up in Enrique's face. "What exactly are you doing with my girlfriend?" he demanded to know. "Girlfriend?" Jono jumped to her feet. "You pig! You get away from me!" she screamed. Troy's tone and demeanor quickly changed. "Jono... it was just a misunderstanding. Look, you and I are good together, we need each other," he pleaded. Many of the people standing in the area turned their attention toward the commotion.

"Need each other? Are you mental? I'm pretty sure you need me, but I definitely don't need you! I don't want to be anywhere near you, and I definitely don't want to be on this ship with you. Get away from me, so help me..." Jono was way beyond pissed. Troy reached out and grabbed her arm, hard. Jono stepped right up to him. "What? Are you going to hit me again?" she lashed out. There were many gasps: Enrique turned and looked at Jono's face, then he turned back and looked at Troy. Troy laughed. "Yeah right!" he scoffed at Enrique. Without a second's hesitation Enrique reached from the floor and gave Troy a right cross hard to his face. Troy dropped to the ground, out cold.

Enrique was shaking off the pain in his hand. Many people including Maxwell and Fernando came running up. "What happened?" Maxwell looked at Jono; Fernando looked at Enrique. "I had to defend the lady's honor." Jono stepped up and took Enrique's arm. "Enrique is the perfect gentleman," she smiled. Maxwell started laughing. Fernando looked at Jono. "I am so sorry. Are you alright?"

he asked sincerely. "Yes, I'm fine. Thanks to Enrique," she added. "Take this man away!" Fernando commanded his security. "You guys, come sit with me where I can watch you!" he jokingly demanded. "Drinks! We need drinks!" Fernando yelled at the top of his lungs. Everyone cheered.

The next morning, late morning, while Jono was having breakfast in one of the hotel restaurants with a few of her staff, Maxwell showed up. The group opened up a seat next to Jono so he could sit down. "Well, that was easy," he said to Jono. "What was easy?" she smiled. "Troy. I didn't have to do anything. I didn't have to ask any favors," he explained, trying not to laugh. Jono moved to the edge of her seat. "I don't understand," she told him. "Troy's eye is so swollen and black and blue, the ad agency had no choice: they sent him home." Now he let out a quiet laugh. Jono wanted to smile but refrained. "He got what he deserved."

Jono was never worried about it anyway, there was no way the magazine or the ad agency would have kept Troy around if she asked, but to have it end this way felt like closure to Jono. She smiled. "Thank you, Max." "Don't thank me, thank Enrique!" Everyone laughed. "Yes, thank you, Enrique!" Jono held up her hands like she was thanking God.

The photo shoot went well, really well. They finished in only three days. Everything cooperated, the weather, the equipment - it all went very smoothly. Jono couldn't be happier with the results: she loved every shot. The next day she did a television interview with a cable fashion network, one of Fernando's companies. Maxwell was like a proud father watching his Jono fielding so many questions like a pro. Then the interviewer threw Jono a question out of left field. "Jono, the whole world knows you almost drowned in Hawaii several weeks back. That had to be pretty scary for you?" she asked. Jono didn't know where this was going, and didn't like it. All press were told upfront not to broach the subject, ever. Jono looked over at Maxwell.

He held up his hands suggesting he had no idea what she should do. "Jono?" the interviewer asked.

"Yes. You're right, it was very scary." Just as Jono was about to change the subject, the interviewer threw in another question.

"We understand by good authority that it was a random beach bum who saved your life?" Jono almost fell out of her chair. She gave the interviewer a look that a tiger might give its prey just before the fatal bite. Jono had no idea what to say or how to respond. She paused. Jono was anything but weak and could not be easily intimidated. She sat straight up in her chair.

"Clare, I am not here today to talk to you about my personal life, nor will I ever talk to anyone about my experience in Hawaii. I'm here to talk about the shoot, fashion and anything else in those two categories you want to talk to me about. Ask me again about my personal life or what happened to me in Hawaii, and I'll make sure this is your last day here at Fashion World Network." Maxwell about jumped out of his skin. "Perfect!" he muttered to himself. Jono caught the all-powerful interviewer so off guard she had to cut to a commercial. Jono stood up and gently set her microphone on the chair. The interviewer walked over to Jono as she was stepping off the stage. "I was only doing my job!" she yelled loudly. Jono didn't even slow down, she walked directly over to Maxwell and together they walked out of the studio. "Okay, that was, like, amazing!" Maxwell spouted as they stepped outside. Jono looked at him and smiled.

They jumped in the car and quickly headed back to the hotel. Jono, as per usual, was met by a large crowd waiting out front. She elegantly and professionally stepped right up to the group so they could take photographs. She smiled, posed and then thanked them. Maxwell and the entourage entered the hotel. Jono grabbed Maxwell by the arm, "Can I talk to you?" she asked. "Of course." Maxwell shooed the others away. He and Jono went into one of the bars. They found a quiet, dark booth and sat down.

"Honestly, Jono, I am so sorry about what happened, but man, you were great!" he started.

"Thanks, but that's not why I need to talk to you."

"Oh, okay."

"Tomorrow when you go home I'm not going with you," she told him with a straight face. Maxwell looked befuddled.

"I decided I want to stay for a few more days, a week, actually," she explained. Maxwell was really confused, and getting upset.

"Jono, I haven't scheduled any security or escorts, I haven't made any other flight or hotel arrangements... Why? Why are you staying?" he asked, completely flustered.

"I know, I'm sorry. But I've got everything taken care of," she assured him. "I wanted to handle everything myself, it's important to me. This is just something I want to do, I need a little break... from everything."

"Is it me?" he asked in as concerned a voice as Jono had ever heard.

"No, Max, no. This has nothing to do with you. I love you... you're my best friend."

Maxwell was scared: Jono could see it in his face.

"This has nothing to do with you or your job, I promise." She leaned over and hugged him. Their drinks showed up at the table. Jono lifted her glass, and Maxwell lifted his. "To a successful shoot!" she announced. Maxwell reciprocated.

"This doesn't have anything to do with Enrique, does it? Because..." Jono started to laugh hard.

"Oh my God, no! Listen, don't worry about it, don't worry about me. I'll see you in New York in a week." Maxwell grumbled something under his breath.

"Sure. Don't worry." He reluctantly smiled. "Sometimes you make me nuts, you know that?" he half-smiled.

"Yup! But then that's one of the reasons you love me."

Early the next morning Jono's crew was packed and ready to go. While they waited for the cars Maxwell took a quick detour up to

Jono's room. He lightly knocked, then went in. Maxwell always had a spare key to Jono's room no matter where they were. He was surprised to see Jono sitting on the couch drinking some coffee.

"What are you doing up so early?"

"I couldn't sleep. Want some coffee?"

"No thank you, I've got to get back downstairs. The cars will be here shortly." Jono nodded. "I see you're all packed?" he questioned. "Did you change your mind?" He smiled inquisitively. Jono smiled back.

"No, I'm just changing locations."

"Jono..." Maxwell was interrupted.

"Max, I know what you're going to say. I promise, I will be fine," she reassured him. She got up from the couch, walked over and hugged him hard. "Please, don't worry," she squeezed his cheek. "Now get going!" She smiled. "Please call me when you land."

"Fine," he grunted. "Be safe... Call me if you need anything."

"I will." Jono had to nearly push Maxwell out of the door. She walked to the balcony and went out. She took in a deep breath of the early morning air. "Freedom!"

Jono finished packing up her bags: she only had two, the rest of her onslaught of luggage went with Maxwell to Los Angeles. She tied her hair up as tight as she could, then wrapped her head in a scarf. She waited for about an hour for the craziness downstairs to calm down. Then she decided it should be safe to go. Thankfully her hairdresser played a good stand-in for Jono when needed. The paparazzi would follow her to the airport and they would think it was Jono getting on the plane. No one would be the wiser until the plane landed in LA. They used this trick all the time so Jono could move about safely and as much as possible unnoticed.

Jono took a second scarf and wrapped it around her shoulders, covering part of her face. She got off the elevator. The lobby was nearly bare, then she hustled out a back entrance. A car was waiting for her. "Are you going to be okay, miss? Wouldn't you rather I get you a driver?" the hotel assistant manager asked. "Thank you very much, but I'll be fine." A bellman set her luggage in the back of the small car and Jono drove off. She was so happy and excited. This would be an adventure like nothing else Jono had never done. She got the chills thinking about it. She was actually amazed Maxwell let her go. She quickly looked into her rear-view mirror to see if anyone was following her: they weren't. This would not be below Maxwell: he would do anything to protect her. The streets were small, mostly covered in cobblestones, and Jono loved it. There were very few cars on the road: it was a Saturday and still early. Once she was clear of the city, Jono pulled the car over. She took out her phone and programmed in her destination. "Two hours and fifteen minutes." She was exhilarated. She put the car in gear and drove off into the countryside.

Two hours later, Jono pulled into a small town. "So beautiful," she thought. She stopped to top off her gas tank and get a drink. The station owner came out to help. At first he spoke to her in Spanish, but quickly changed to English. "You speak English very well." Jono was surprised.

"Gracias, American television," he told her. Jono laughed. "Yes, I see you on the television all the time," he said.

"You know me?" She was caught completely off guard.

"Si, si, you are the Jono, right?"

Jono smiled. "Yes. I am the Jono."

The man turned off the pump. "Where are you headed?" he inquired.

"Oh just a cottage up the road: you know, a little holiday," she told him.

"Ah, Si, si. Gracias."

"Gracias, señor." Jono got back in the car and waved at the man as she pulled out onto the road.

It was such a beautiful country: rolling hills, trees and flowers everywhere. Large farms covered the landscape. "Turn here," the phone told her. Jono turned up a steep, narrow dirt road. She drove a few more minutes till she came to a cottage sitting by itself on the hill, surrounded by many plants and large old trees. The front looked like something out of a child's storybook: there were flowers everywhere. Jono pulled alongside the house and parked next to the two other cars that were there. She got out of the car, but before she could do anything else she stood and stared at the stunning view.

"It's not Hawaii, but it will have to do!" Jono turned to see Mike walking toward her holding his arms out wide.

"MIKE!" Jono ran and jumped into his arms. Mike spun her around. Jono kissed Mike all over his head and face, then she reached his mouth. She devoured his lips, kissing him with every ounce of passion she had in her body. Mike gently set her down. He held her face in his hands. "I am so happy to see you." Jono socked him. "Ow, what was that for?" he smiled. "That was for dumping me in Hawaii!" They both laughed and then hugged.

"Come on, there's someone I want you to meet." Mike grabbed her hand and walked her into the cottage. Jono was immediately bowled over by the smells.

"Oh my God, what is that?!" Jono yelped.

"That's lunch!" a lovely older Spanish woman announced as she entered the room. Jono was struck by how beautiful she was: small in stature, older, maybe sixty-five or seventy. But such a beautiful face, with bright brown eyes.

"Jono, I'd like you to meet Mrs. Duran, the owner of this house."

"Oh no, please, call me Carmen, I insist." Jono walked over to her and shook her hand.

"You are so beautiful," Jono told her. Carmen nearly blushed. "Really," Jono insisted.

"You are too kind to such an old woman."

"I told her the same thing." Mike smiled.

"Thank you for letting us use your beautiful home, it is truly like a storybook," Jono told the woman.

"I lived in this old house for nearly fifty years, now people want to pay me to stay here - funny. But I like meeting new people, I like making them happy. It's good," Carmen paused. "Okay! That's it, lunch is on the stove, food is in the cupboards and wine is on the counter. I will be back in a few days to check on you two," Carmen told them.

"Thank you." Mike walked her to the door.

Carmen stopped and turned back to Jono. She held up a finger and pointed at her. "Don't break the bed, it's very old," Carmen smiled then walked out. Now Jono was the one blushing.

Jono and Mike never made it to the bedroom, or the kitchen, at least for several hours. They locked bodies right there on the floor and never came up for air. Jono didn't think, she just was. Every part of her was committed to Mike, physically, emotionally and even spiritually. It was two hours of pure passion. Mike and Jono couldn't get enough of each other. Finally their bodies gave out: sweaty and exhausted they lay on the floor, side-by-side, staring into each other's eyes.

"You know I love you," Mike said softly.

"I know."

"Do you think I'm nuts?" he asked.

Jono smiled. "To be in love with me... yes."

"Jono, is Maxwell right? Am I complicating your life, am I bad for you?" he questioned sincerely.

Jono leaned in and got as close as she could. "Just as bad as I am for you." She kissed him hard and long, then rolled him on his back. Jono got her second wind and took over, much to Mike's content.

Sometime later, after they had both showered, they finally sat at the kitchen table to eat the food Carmen left for them. "Oh man, this is so good!" Jono exclaimed, unfemininely stuffing her face with pasta. They spent the next couple days completely engrossed in each other, never venturing far from the cottage. They talked, went on walks, drank great wine, ate great food, and made love as often as their bodies would allow. Carmen stopped by once, only for a few minutes, to drop off some precooked meals and more wine. "Love is in the air!" she exclaimed as she whisked back out the front door, waving as she did.

On the third night, Jono and Mike decided to go into town to try something different, more to give their bodies a break and to get out of the house. Right in the middle of the town square they found a quaint cafe-bar: they decided to go in. The cafe was surprisingly busy with what appeared to be only locals. "This must be the spot," Mike told Jono. A young man helped them to a table that just opened next to one of the front windows. "This place is great!" Jono said loudly, trying to speak over the other voices; Mike smiled in agreement. They ordered wine and the house speciality, croquettes, a delightful Spanish appetizer. They both decided on gazpacho for dinner.

A man was playing a guitar in the corner of the café. He was really good; many people were laughing, some were singing; it looked like everyone was having a good time. It was a very festive atmosphere. Jono thought maybe it was a holiday or something; it turned out this was just a regular night. Mike and Jono were deep in conversation, enjoying their food and wine, when Jono was approached by a young woman who was carrying a baby on her hip. In very broken English she spoke to Jono. "You're Jono, the model, yes?" she asked. Jono looked at the woman then the child, and smiled. "Yes, I'm Jono." Jono reached out her hand to shake, but the woman suddenly turned away, and yelled out something in Spanish very loudly, getting most everyone's attention. Neither Jono nor Mike had any clue what she said; the only thing Jono heard was her name three or four times. Jono looked at Mike. She was starting to panic, then all of a sudden everyone in the cafe started chanting, "Jono! Jono!", clapping and smiling. Mike looked at Jono. "I think we're okay," he smiled.

Food and bottles of wine flowed to their table: everyone in the cafe wanted to buy the young couple a drink. The owner came over and introduced himself. His English was terrible, but right behind him came two large plates of desserts. "Oh, man! Look at that!" Mike laughed. "I am looking at it, and I can't touch it!" Jono said, making a pouty face. The night rolled on for hours. It became a party: several more men showed up with instruments and the dancing began. Just as Mike was thinking about it, a very old Spaniard reached out his hand to Jono, requesting a dance. Jono gracefully accepted. It wasn't long till the oldest woman in the cafe asked Mike to dance. Jono and Mike were being passed from person to person, spinning, singing, laughing and with lots of hugs. Jono had never had so much fun in her life.

The next morning or actually early afternoon, Jono and Mike woke to the onset of massive headaches. Mike heard some noise in the kitchen, so he went to check it out. Carmen was cooking; she smiled when she saw Mike holding his head. "I heard you had some fun last night," she teased.

"A little too much, I think." He sat down at the table and picked up the cup of coffee that was sitting there for him.

"Not to worry, I've got the perfect cure," Carmen told him.

"That smells really good, but I don't think I can eat anything," he explained.

"I know. But this will make you feel better, then you will be hungry."

"Whatever you say. Anything to make this headache go away." Jono came walking into the kitchen holding her head. She looked like she'd been standing in front of a giant fan, her hair was going everywhere, her face was pale, and she looked like she was going to be sick any second. She sat down at the table across from Mike.

"Good morning," Carmen cheerfully said. Jono tried to lift her head but she was afraid to. "Morning." Barely audible. Carmen set two bowls of soup down on the table. "Eat this," she told them.

"Oh, I can't." Jono's head was spinning. She started to get up, thinking she was going to be sick, then slowly sat back down.

"Just a sip, you'll see," Carmen told them both. Each of them picked up a spoon. Mike took a sip of the brew, then another, then a third. "This is really good." Jono reluctantly followed Mike's cue. She barely got the spoon to her lips: she took a very small sip. She nodded in agreement. Then she ate a spoonful. In minutes Mike was nearly done and asked for more. By her third or fourth spoonful, color started to come back to Jono's face. She sat up. "Carmen, this is amazing. I feel so much better. I can actually feel my headache going away."

"Very old family recipe, cures everything, especially what you have," she joked. "Tomorrow is your last day here, no?"

"Yes," Mike said, not wanting to admit it.

"Yes. So I have packed you some meals and you can have a picnic up on the mountain and watch the sunset."

"On no. No hiking for me!" Jono blurted out.

"Yes, it's easy and not far. You'll see." She looked at Mike. "I drew you a map." She pointed to a piece of paper on the table. Mike nodded. "Okay, I've got to go. I'll see you in the morning?"

"Yes," Mike assured her. Carmen kissed Jono on the head then went out the door. Mike looked at Jono: they both looked so beat-up. Jono started to laugh, then Mike. "You ready to go on a hike?" Mike asked. Jono burst out laughing, then abruptly stopped. "Ow," she said as she grabbed her head.

Later that afternoon they both sat on the couch, staring at the basket Carmen packed for them. "I'm feeling better. Are you feeling better?" Mike asked Jono. Jono nodded. "I am."

"Should we do this?" Mike smiled.

"I'm game if you are."

"Last night, last adventure," he told her. They slowly got up. Mike picked up the basket, Jono picked up the blanket Carmen set out, and they went to one of the cars. Mike put the basket and blanket in the back seat, then they drove down the dirt road to the main road. They didn't have to go far when they came to the turn that was indicated on Carmen's map: another small dirt road that went nearly straight up. Mike slowly worked his way up the windy road, climbing the whole time. Then the road came to a stop. "Where'd the road go?" Jono asked. "I guess this is it." Mike set the car brake as hard as he could, then got out of the car. "You're going to want to see this," he called out to Jono who was reaching into the back seat to retrieve the blanket. Jono got out and turned toward the back of the car. "Wow! Now I understand why Carmen didn't want us to miss this."

There was a small foot trail off to the left. Carmen was right: it was a short, easy hike. Jono lay out the blanket under a big tree and sat down. Mike put down the basket and sat next to her. "Wine?" Jono whacked him hard. Mike laughed. It couldn't have been any more beautiful or romantic. They sipped on the bottled water, holding each other tight; the sun was slowly setting into the horizon.

"Jono… what happens now?" Mike asked, interrupting the quiet. Jono sat up and looked at him.

"I've been focused on this week for so long, I haven't really thought about it." They sat quietly watching the sun take its last breath before slipping into the sea. It started to get dark fast.

"We'd better go," Mike suggested as he stood. Jono grabbed his arm and pulled him back down. She sat in Mike's lap and wrapped her long legs around him.

"I've never been in this place before, I'm not sure what to do," she confided to Mike. She took both of his hands and gently kissed them. She looked at Mike. She pursed her lips tightly then slowly changed them to a smile. "I love you," she admitted confidently. For the first time in Jono's life she knew this was real, she knew these feelings were coming from her heart. Mike smiled. "I know." Jono whacked him again, hard on the arm. "Is it always going to be like this, you hitting me when you're happy? What do I do if you get mad?" he joked.

They packed up the car and drove back to the cottage. Jono went into the bedroom and starting packing. Mike loaded the cars: they had a long drive and needed to start early. Jono called Mike to come sit with her at the kitchen table.

"I have to be in New York the day after tomorrow. Why don't you come with me?"

"New York? I don't know, Jono. I have a lot of work I need to get back to in Hawaii." He smiled. He was already holding Jono's hands: he was prepared. Jono laughed. "But seriously, Jono, do you think this is a good idea - for you, I mean?"

"For me... it will be awesome! We'll have so much fun. I am worried about you, though."

"Me? Why?"

"I don't think you're going to like my reality, it can be rough. Trust me, the minute we get on the plane together in Madrid, your privacy goes out the window, your picture will be everywhere. You will be a part of my life, and I'm not sure you're going to like it."

"Yeah... I understand. Being part of your life, that does sound like a drag," he smiled. Jono thought about it, but didn't hit him. "The truth is, I wish I could just whisk you away and get lost together, like this week. But I know that's not possible. So I know, if I want to be with you, I guess I have to *be with you*." Jono gave him a big smooch followed by a smile so big it made her face hurt.

Mike and Jono had the cars packed and were just about to leave when Carmen pulled up. "Good morning!" Jono sang out. "Good morning to you. You look like you're all set." "We are," Mike told her. "And Carmen, thank you for the suggestion: watching the sunset last night was amazing," Jono told her. Carmen smiled.

"What's this?" she asked, pointing to the cars. "Aren't you both going to Madrid?"

"We are. But we came in two different cars," Mike explained.

"Pish. That's just crazy. I'll have my sons return one of them for you. This way you can drive together. This is much better."

"Really? You would do that for us?" Jono asked.

"Of course. This way you can spend more time together. This is good, no?"

"Yes. Very good," Mike smiled. They said their goodbyes and drove off together in one car.

Jono wasn't exaggerating even a little. The minute Jono and Mike entered the airport in Madrid holding hands, people were swarming all over them. Thankfully security was prepared, and literally ran them up to a secure area in the airport where they could wait for their flight unmolested. By the time they got back down into the main terminal, the media were waiting for them. Cameras, bright lights beaming on them, following them all the way to the security area. At one point, Jono decided to stop and address some of the questions. Mike let go of her hand, but Jono didn't let go of his.

Jono posed for a few pictures, then volunteered to answer questions. But she only got the same one: "Jono, who are you wearing?" Jono smiled, then turned toward Mike.

"This is Mike," she smiled proudly.

"Who is Mike?" a reporter asked. Mike chuckled; Jono nudged him.

"Mike is my boyfriend and my hero," she announced. Mike wasn't expecting this, but he figured Jono knew what she was doing. A few reporters tried to ask Mike some questions but Jono deflected all of them.

"What do you mean by 'hero'?" someone asked.

"Mike saved my life… in more ways than one," she told the salivating group.

"Mike, Mike! What does Jono mean? How did you save her life?" yelled one reporter insisting on details. Once again Jono deflected.

"It was Mike who pulled me from the ocean in Hawaii: he saved my life, he kept me from drowning." That set off a firestorm of questions. Jono gave the nod to one of the security men, then just like that Jono and Mike were rushed to their plane and boarded.

"Oh boy," Mike let out as he sat in his seat. Jono looked at him and made a face. "That was easy," she explained.

"Oh good. Drinks!" Mike yelled out. Jono started cracking up.

While Jono and Mike were in flight a lot of people back in the States were catching them on the evening and entertainment news, including Maxwell. He sat in his hotel room staring at his television with his mouth hanging open. "Holy shit!" He quickly called the whole staff into his room. Everyone was stunned. Back at Mike's firehouse in Denver, his old crew were glued to the television. "That's Mike! Holy shit! I can't believe it, that's Captain Mike!"

Jono and Mike slept most of the long flight home. After landing, Jono asked Mike to wait until all of the other passengers were off the plane. Jono was used to traveling with her entourage, especially her make-up assistant and hairdresser. She was freaking out a little. "What's wrong?" Mike asked.

"Ah... There's going to be hundreds of reporters and photographers waiting for us out there. Look at me, I'm a wreck!"

Mike laughed. "Not on your worst day!" But Jono wasn't smiling; she frantically dug through her carry-on. "Give me a minute." Mike walked to the cabin door and talked to the stewardesses who were waiting there. "Okay, come on, we're good," he told Jono as he reached for her hand.

"Good? What do you mean? How are we good?" Mike turned to Jono and gave her a Jono look. Jono smiled. "Okay... we're good." They walked to the cabin door where two security guards were waiting. Instead of walking down the gangway to the terminal, security walked Jono and Mike down the external stairs to the ground and ran them into the terminal through an employee entrance. They went up a flight of stairs, maneuvered through some back hallways, and emerged in the airline's private club where Maxwell and the rest of Jono's crew were waiting. Jono grabbed Mike around the neck. "Brilliant! You are brilliant!" The she kissed him on the forehead. "I love this man!" she announced proudly to the group. Maxwell stood with a big smile on his face: he was excited to see Jono, but he was so happy to see her so happy.

Everyone crowded around Mike and Jono: they all wanted a closer look. Almost everyone gave Mike a supportive hug. Mike wasn't ready for it, but went with it. Maxwell beelined straight to Jono. He crushed her with a full-on man hug. Jono yelped. He looked her in the eyes. "I guess we have some catching up to do?" he joked. "I guess we do," Jono smiled. Then Maxwell turned to Mike. "Mike," he acknowledged rather coldly. Mike smiled. "Maxwell, it's a pleasure to see you again," Mike told him sincerely.

"Oh come here, surfer boy!" Maxwell smiled, grabbed Mike and gave him a monster hug, then kissed him on the cheek; Mike was stunned. Jono laughed uncontrollably while the others clapped. Mike quickly moved back to Jono's side.

After thirty minutes with hair and make-up, Jono, Mike and Maxwell exited the club, and, with a great deal of security, headed for the airport exit. Out front there were so many cameras, reporters and looky-loos the airport had to close down two lanes of traffic. They quickly made their way to the waiting cars; Jono waved but took no questions.

"So, kids, how was Spain?" Maxwell asked once they were safely in the car. "Do we have pictures?"

"We had a blast and yes we do." Jono handed Maxwell her phone. Maxwell sat quietly scrolling through the many photographs; every once in a while he would chuckle or comment, "Oh this is beautiful."

For months Jono and Mike were inseparable. Mike traveled with Jono everywhere. It was often awkward for Mike, being around the fashion process; he tried to stay away as much as possible so Jono could concentrate on her work. It was the right thing for both of them. But every chance they could, no matter what the job or where it was, they would either go a few days early or stay a few days late to sneak away to be alone. For the most part, it worked. Once in a while Jono would get spotted and they would find themselves on the run. Mike hated it; Jono loved it because she wasn't bearing all the pressure alone anymore; she actually thought it was fun. They traveled all over the world together, including several exotic locations. On one such trip to Fiji, Jono and Mike finally got to surf again. Jono was up and surfing on her first try. For Mike, watching Jono surf was an emotional experience. The way her face changed, she was excited, having fun, but trying so hard to be better. When she was surfing, her senses were fully loaded; Mike respected that. After one pretty bad wipeout, Jono decided to take a break. She and Mike sat down on the beach and relaxed.

"Looks like there's some good ones coming in," Mike pointed back out to the water.

"Oh wow. Looks like I got out just in time," Jono smiled. "I bet these are perfect for you, though!" she told him, and Mike nodded. With all the surfing they had done together, Jono had only seen Mike surf a couple of times, and always on the same baby waves that Jono was learning on. "Come on. Go out, I'd love to see you *really* surf." Mike didn't hesitate, he jumped to his feet, kissed Jono, grabbed the surfboard and ran for the water. Right away, Jono was impressed; Mike paddled out like a pro, fast and commanding, sailing over the waves with ease. In less than a minute he was behind the breakwater. Mike sat up on the board and waved to Jono; Jono stood up to see better and waved back. Moments later, Mike was paddling for a wave, a big one. Jono was very happy she was standing on the beach and not in the water. Jono watched Mike paddle hard; the wave quickly started to form behind him, and he paddled harder. Seconds later he was up, and Jono screamed with excitement. Mike's ride was awe-inspiring to Jono. He moved up and down the wave, using every part of it, then he charged the top of the wave, and at the last second right at the crest he made a hundred and eighty degree turn, spraying water high into the blue sky, then surfed back down the face of the wave. Jono was jumping up and down on the beach, screaming at the top of her lungs, "Go Mike!" Mike came in after that ride: he was exhausted.

"That was unbelievable!" Jono tackled him just as he set down the surfboard.

"Thanks. It's been a while. That was really fun."

Watching Mike working the wave, his power and grace did something to Jono. She grabbed his hand and pulled him back up; she had a look in her eyes. Mike tried to reach for a bottle of water but Jono was tugging with all her might. She forced him to run with her to their small private cottage on the beach; Jono was naked before they were even in the door. Mike was wet and exhausted, but his energy came back to him in an instant. Jono nearly tore his suit off of him, then threw him on the bed. Mike didn't say a word, he only smiled. Jono's insides were raging with desire, she attacked Mike like he was her last meal.

Jono was happier than she'd ever been in her life. She was at the top of her game, she was with the man she loved, she was living a dream, her dream. Jono understood this and didn't take it for granted. She was scared to even think about how happy she was: she was so afraid of it changing.

For Mike it was a little different. He loved being with Jono:, she kept him hopping, always making him laugh no matter where they were or what was going on. But the intensity of the limelight, the parties, the men and women constantly fawning all over Jono were starting to wear on him. He did his best not to show it, especially when Jono was close by. At interviews he tried to stay clear, but often Jono would pull him in; he'd smile but would never answer any questions. In the earliest part of the relationship, Mike was asked to be interviewed for major entertainment magazines and several television daytime shows to discuss the 'rescue'. He always declined. A number of times he and Jono showed up on the cover of some of these magazines anyway: "Jono's Hero" was the most common headline. Mike hated the attention but still bought himself extra copies.

Mike and Maxwell practically became best friends: they had a common bond and unique perspective that only they could understand. It turned out that Mike was a major help to Maxwell when it came to dealing with Jono: Mike was the perfect buffer between himself and Jono. And when he needed to approach Jono with something uncomfortable or something that he knew would make her mad, he'd go to Mike first. Together they became a team. Jono loved it: her man and her best friend in the world were friends. Maxwell and Mike long forgot their early differences and only focused on Jono. Mike took his health and conditioning very seriously: he had the body to prove it. His health habits had had a great influence on Jono; she ate much better, drank less, and worked out every once in a while. Mike had tried countless times to get Maxwell involved but to no avail. "No it's okay, I'm good," he would always say. "I don't want to be too attractive!"

A CHANGE IN TIDES

On one of the rare visits home to Los Angeles, Mike showed up at Maxwell's office to pick up Jono to take her to a movie; so hard to do, but always so much fun. From the second he walked in the door he knew something was wrong. Maxwell sat on a couch in the foyer, Jono was pacing back and forth in front of him, and Mike could tell she had been crying.

"Jono, what's the matter?" He walked up to her and put his arms around her. Jono jerked her body, throwing Mike's arms off of her and walked away, sobbing. Mike was confused. He looked at Maxwell: Maxwell didn't even look at him.

"Jono, what's wrong? Maybe I can help?" he asked sincerely. He reached out again to touch her.

"I'm pretty sure you helped enough!" Jono yelled at him getting right in his face. Mike was shocked: he'd never scene or heard Jono so upset.

"What? What's wrong?" Mike's brain was racing, trying to think if he done or said anything that might have caused this; he came up with nothing. He looked at Maxwell. Maxwell shrugged his shoulders.

Mike tried a third time to approach Jono. She hit his hand out of the air, totally catching Mike off guard. She was pissed.

"You know what, Mike... I think you need to go!" she told him angrily. Mike was paralyzed; he didn't know what to say or do. Maxwell stood.

"Jono..."

"NO! He needs to go and he needs to go right now!" she barely paused. "In fact, Mike, why don't you and I take a little break? I hear Hawaii calling you!" She pointed at the door.

"Jono!" Mike exclaimed. "What the hell? What did I do? You can at least tell me that!"

"No! Do not say another word." She gave Mike a look that would scare any man. "Now!" she yelled. Mike looked at Maxwell: he didn't say a word or give Mike any kind of sign. Mike shook his head in disgust, turned and walked out; he didn't know what else to do. *After she calms down, then I will be able to figure this out,* he thought.

Mike went back to Jono's house. He waited and waited till he fell asleep on her couch. She never came home: there were no calls, texts or voicemails. Mike woke up early. He tried calling Jono first right away: no answer. He texted her at least ten times: no response. He called and texted Maxwell all morning: nothing. He had no idea what to do or who to contact, and then the front doorbell rang.

"Jono?" Mike called out. He ran to the door and opened it: he stepped back, surprised and disappointed. He expected it to be someone different. "Mr. Johnson?" The man in a black suit asked him. "Yes, I'm Mike Johnson." "I'm here to take you to the airport, sir," he explained. Mike stepped outside; a black town car was waiting. Mike was disappointed, shocked and hurt, and he didn't understand. *Why is she doing this?* he questioned himself. "I need a few minutes," he told the driver. "Yes, sir, no problem. I'll just be waiting in the car." Mike walked to the bedroom. He tried to call Jono as he did. No answer, so he left a message.

"Jono, I guess you weren't kidding: there's a car here for me. So I'm leaving, I'm going home. I don't have any idea what's going on or what I did to make you feel you need to do this." As he spoke he started to get pissed off. "You're being unfair, not talking to me at all, not explaining what's going on or what the hell I did to make you so angry. Just leaving me hanging in the dark: is this fair? This isn't how I thought we were. I thought we had something special, I thought we talked about everything?" He paused and his voice became somber. "I hate myself for not knowing, not being able to help you, but it appears you've made up your mind. I'll leave you alone, maybe some day, when you feel up to it, you can explain all of this to me. That would be nice." Then he abruptly hung up the phone.

Mike sat on the plane for six hours, thinking, questioning, trying to remember if there could have been anything he said or did. Not even necessarily to Jono. *Maybe I pissed off Maxwell somehow,* he questioned. He wasn't coming up with anything. *What the heck, man?* He kept rubbing his head, and squeezing his face, frustrated beyond words. His thoughts eventually led him to question the relationship at all. *Maybe she doesn't really love me? Maybe it was all about fun for her? Maybe she found someone new?* All of these thoughts circled around Mike's mind for six hours. *Why wouldn't she just tell me?*

Mike landed in Honolulu, in a way happy to be home. He was walking down to baggage claim not thinking about anything; he was exhausted from trying to figure out why he was home in the first place, when he saw a big crowd of people and reporters standing outside the airport doors. "Must be another celebrity," he thought. He looked at his phone: no calls or texts from Jono or Maxwell: no calls or texts from anyone. He grabbed his backpack and luggage and proceeded out the door. He purposely walked to the far exit to avoid the crowd. As he passed through the sliding doors, someone yelled out his name. "Mike!" "There he is!" someone else yelled. Then the mob of people and cameras ran toward him. Mike stood there stunned.

Cameras going off, lights in his eyes, microphones in his face. Questions were being screamed out so loudly and at such a rapid pace that Mike couldn't understand any of them. He was surrounded on all sides: he couldn't move if he wanted to. He finally got frustrated and raised his hands over his head. "Stop!" he yelled. Amazingly everyone quieted down. "What do you want?" he asked sternly. The crowd went right back to full volume and intensity. Mike gave up and tried to move through the crowd, but he actually had nowhere to go, no car, no one expecting him. "Awe, man, I can't stand here and wait for a taxi!" He knew he couldn't walk, and no way was he taking a bus. He was actually starting to get claustrophobic; he got shoved really hard from the back, he turned and was ready to hit someone when he saw it was a woman who was pushed by the crowd.

"Mikala!" someone yelled out. "Mikala!" Someone was calling Mike's name in Hawaiian. He turned toward the voice, it was Kale. Mike was never so happy to see a familiar face. "Kale!" They embraced. "Thank God you're here!" Mike told him. Kale pulled him from the crowd, and waiting in a nearby truck was Kaleen. She was waving frantically. The crowd followed closely behind, still desperate for Mike to answer their questions. Kale threw Mike's gear in the back and they both got in the truck. The crowd surrounded the truck; many stood in front of it. Kaleen laid on the horn, the people slowly started to move away. One aggressive male reporter put his face right up to Mike's window and yelled, "How do you feel about what you did to Jono?" Mike looked at him with a face of terror. Kaleen hit the gas and they raced away.

"What did that guy say? He asked me about what I did to Jono, right?" Mike asked his only friends. "I'm so glad you're home!" Kaleen told him.

"I'm sorry. I'm such an idiot. Thank you, you guys. You really saved me back there. I came out of the airport and suddenly I was mobbed by all these reporters. I had no idea what to do. Thank God you came along..." Mike paused. *Why did you come along?* he asked.

"How did you and all those people even know I was coming today?" he started to question.

"The news," Kale spoke up.

"The news? Why would I be on the news?"

"Michael, you just got home to a rather unpleasant welcoming committee; let's get you home, have some lunch and we'll catch up on everything. We're excited to hear about what's been going on with you," Kaleen suggested.

"Okay, yeah, sorry. That sounds great, thank you," Mike tried to smile, but he was at a loss. *What did that guy mean, what I did to Jono?* he asked himself. Mike took a deep breath, enjoying the familiar fragrances. "It's good to be back."

Kaleen pulled up in front of Dan's house and parked the truck. They all got out. Kaleen walked straight over to Mike and gave him a big hug. "Come on, let's go inside," she suggested. Mike followed. Kale grabbed Mike's bags, then followed. Mike was red with frustration.

"Kaleen, what did you mean about me being on the news? I don't understand," Mike asked as he sat at the kitchen counter. Kaleen poured him some tea. Mike took a big drink. "Man, I missed that!" he smiled. Kaleen smiled with satisfaction. Kale came in and sat down next to Mike. He put his hand on his shoulder. "How're you doing?" Kale asked sincerely.

"Well, to be honest with you, I'm not sure. My life was fun, crazy but fun. I was traveling the world with the woman I love then, two days ago, Jono went crazy on me. She kicked me out of her life with no explanation, I get home and I'm mobbed by people who apparently think I did something to her." Mike leaned on the counter and put his fist on his forehead. "It's nuts... I have no idea what happened."

Kaleen reached to the other side of the counter where she picked up a newspaper, and set it down in front of Mike. "What's this?" he asked.

"Go to the entertainment section," she told him. Mike opened the paper then flipped through the pages until he reached the right section. In bold print across the entire page:

Nude photos of Jono go viral!

Below the caption was a photograph of Jono lying on what looked like a beach towel, completely naked with all the important parts blurred out. "What the hell?" Mike looked up at Kaleen. "Read on," she suggested. Mike read the article: he got into the second paragraph where the article quoted Jono's manager, Maxwell. "To release these photos of Jono without Jono's permission, for financial gain and to purposely try to hurt Jono, is inexcusable and unforgivable. This borders on evil. Jono is so hurt and upset by the release of these photographs that she will be taking some time off and will not be doing any interviews. We would prefer that all future questions or requests go through Jono's attorneys."

"Oh my God. This is terrible! But I don't understand, what does this have to do with me?" Mike reacted.

"You should keep reading," Kale told him, pointing at the paper. Mike read on.

Jono's publicist added: "We understand that Jono's friend Mike Johnson is the one who released these photographs. We are all surprised at his actions and deeply hurt and ashamed. Jono has no idea why he would ever do such a thing except for money. Mike Johnson was, well, a beach bum before he met Jono. It turns out Jono was his meal ticket." Mike rumpled up the paper and threw it down on the counter.

"The paper, the news, everyone has been running this story," Kaleen told him. "It was the news that broadcasted you were coming back. I guess the media didn't have any trouble finding out when," Kaleen added. Mike put his hands over his face and leaned back so far on his stool he nearly fell off of it. He looked at Kale, then at Kaleen.

"I didn't do this," he said in a quiet, low tone. Hurt and confused himself, he had no idea what to say. "Why would I do this? I love Jono. I would never do anything to hurt her or embarrass her, ever!" he said, raising his voice.

"Come on, let's sit down," Kaleen suggested. Mike and Kaleen sat on the couch, Kale sat in a chair right next to them. "Mike, we know how much you care about Jono: you never had to say anything, we could see it," Kaleen started. She leaned in closer. Mike could tell she was uncomfortable. "Did you take any nude pictures of Jono?" she asked in nearly a whisper. Mike nodded his head.

"Yes, a few," he shamefully admitted. "We were in Spain, we were out with some local people, we drank a lot. Jono wanted to give me something... you know, special." Mike was red with embarrassment. Mike stood up. "But you know what, I distinctly remember deleting those pictures the next morning. I know I was pretty badly hung over... but I'm sure I did." He sat back down, trying hard to remember.

"Well, how'd they get on the internet then?" Kale asked. Mike looked him straight in the eyes.

"I have no idea."

"Maybe someone got a hold of your phone?" Kale genuinely asked. Mike threw himself deeper into the couch.

"Jono was the only other person to ever touch my phone." Kaleen and Kale sat there quietly, watching Mike hurt himself trying to figure out what happened. "I'm sure I deleted those photographs," Mike mumbled. He turned and looked at Kaleen. "Does Jono know I'm here?"

"No one knows you're here, thankfully. Honestly, I haven't spoken to Jono since you guys left. When Kale and I saw the news, we knew you would be in trouble. That's why we went to the airport, hoping to find you before the news people did." Mike thanked them both again and hugged Kaleen.

"You believe me, don't you?" he asked them both.

"Mike, if we didn't think something was screwy about this whole thing, we wouldn't have showed up at the airport," she told him. "Of course we believe you. I just worry that Jono will not," Kaleen admitted. "Someone managed to get those pictures off your phone. I don't know if we'll ever know who or how... I guess," she added. Mike got up and started walking toward his bags. "Where you going?" Kaleen asked him.

"You guys have already done too much. I should get going."

"Are you crazy?!" Kale yelped at him. "Where are you going to go? The beaches all over Hawaii will be crawling with reporters and paparazzi looking for you."

"Kale's right, Mike. You need to lay low for a while. We'd like it if you stayed here... we want you to stay here." She smiled. Kale nodded in agreement.

"I don't know what to say."

"Mahalo." Kale gave him his answer.

"Yes, Mahalo."

For days Mike basically hid in the house. Kaleen and Kale were right: every once in a while Mike would see someone walking down the beach in front of the house with a camera strung over their necks, stopping people, obviously asking questions. Only at night, with the house lights off, would Mike go out. He swam every night. He wanted to surf so badly, but knew he would be immediately spotted. Being able to talk with Kaleen and Kale helped Mike a lot: they were so supportive and understanding.

In the first couple of days, Mike tried to reach out to Jono; he wanted her to know, if it was *his* fault, it wasn't on purpose and it certainly wasn't for money. Mike couldn't care less about money, but *maybe Jono doesn't know that*. On the second day, he tried to text Maxwell, but the number was disconnected. Then he tried Jono again: the same result. Mike was cut off, there was no way for him to apologize or explain. He was devastated.

It took Mike over a week to get up the nerve to ask Kaleen if he could use the computer: he didn't want to look but he had to. He did a search on Jono: thousands of pages and links came up. Most of the first ones were advertising that they had the nude photos of Jono. Mike wanted to look but he didn't. It hurt too much; he was disgusted at himself. He did check out some of the other links which gave him a great amount of detail about where Jono was and what she was doing. Apparently she was in Australia back at work. "That's good," Mike thought.

After a few weeks of being housebound, Mike couldn't stand it anymore. He had to get out, he needed to go surfing, and he couldn't let himself take advantage of Kaleen and Kale anymore. Kaleen and Kale tried, but Mike had his mind made up. He was going to go find a nice rock somewhere and bury himself under it. He picked up his surfboard, his gear and the pack of food Kaleen had made for him, and headed to the beach. He stopped at the water, turned and looked back at the house: Kaleen and Kale were standing on the deck waving, Kaleen yelling out, "Aloha!" Mike disappeared out of sight.

Jono was miserable and out of control. She yelled and screamed at everyone who came near her, often for no reason - almost always for no *good* reason. Maxwell tried but even he couldn't control Jono anymore. The trip and shoot in Australia went terribly. Thousands of photographs were taken, but the photographer told Maxwell he'd be lucky if he could use one or two of them. Jono started drinking heavily, and not just at night or at parties; she was drinking every chance she could. Maxwell had no choice but to cancel the several television appearances that were scheduled for Jono. She was embarrassing herself and turning herself into a paparazzi dream girl. After weeks of this, even Maxwell couldn't take it anymore: he took action and canceled all future bookings until Jono either got better or quit. The role of being her friend began to outweigh his role as her manager. If she didn't care about ruining her career, then he didn't care.

Back in LA, Jono slept most days, getting up to eat, drink or watch a movie with Maxwell. Maxwell basically moved in with Jono whether she wanted him to or not, and refused to leave no matter how bad some of their fights got. Over time, Jono started to calm down some, enough so that she and Maxwell could talk and have a good cry together. In the end, Jono was still Jono, the young amazing beauty that Maxwell loved.

One morning, Jono came out of her bedroom wearing just her panties, walked to the kitchen and poured herself a cup of coffee. Maxwell sat quietly watching her from the kitchen table.

"What… you're not going to say 'good morning'?" Jono half-smiled.

"Good morning," Maxwell quietly gasped and put a hand to his mouth. "Jono, come over here for a second," he requested.

"What? Why?"

"Please just come here," he said a little more forcefully. Jono picked up her cup of coffee and begrudgingly went over to Maxwell. She stood right in front of him.

"What?"

"Jono, honey… did you swallow a small basketball or something when I wasn't looking?" He smiled and put his hand on her stomach. Jono slapped his hand and backed away.

"What's wrong with you?"

"Me? Have you looked at your stomach lately?" he asked in a little too jolly a way.

"Yeah, okay, so I put on a little weight. I'll get it back off soon enough," she snapped at him.

"Uh… not this weight, you won't," he chuckled.

"Maxwell, seriously! I don't have the patience. I'm pretty sure you don't want to piss me off right now!" she scolded. "I'll lose the weight long before I start working again. I've done it before, no big deal," she scoffed and started to walk out to the family room. Maxwell followed.

"How have you been feeling lately?" he questioned sincerely.

"Seriously? What's with you? You are with me twenty-four-seven, you know exactly how *I'm feeling*," she said, doing the quote sign with her fingers. "Sheesh!" She sat on the couch, folded her legs and continued drinking her coffee. Maxwell sat in a chair across from her.

"You've been feeling sick a lot lately, especially in the mornings, haven't you?" Jono turned on the television, shaking her head at Maxwell like he'd lost his mind. Maxwell got up and went and sat down on the couch next to her. He picked up the remote and turned off the television.

"You're mental, right? Usually it's me, I get that, but now – what? You're paying me back?!" she yelled in a very mean tone. Maxwell looked at her with the most serious face he could.

"When did you have your last period?" he asked as gently as he possible could. Jono started to get up from the couch. Maxwell grabbed her arm and pulled her back down. "Jono, I'm serious. When did you have your last period?" he asked more demanding. Jono could see he was serious. She relented.

"I'm not sure... maybe two, I don't know, might be three months, why?" Maxwell didn't respond. "I'm sure it's stress. I know it's stress; you know my life has been far from perfect lately," she added. Maxwell moved closer to her and put his hand on her leg. He cleared his throat.

"I think you need to take a pregnancy test."

"What!?" Jono erupted from the couch. "Now I know you've lost your mind! You seriously think I'm pregnant! That's a laugh. I haven't even had sex since Mike and that was over..." Jono sat back down. "Oh shit!"

It only took peeing on a stick to confirm Maxwell's hunch. Jono sat on the couch next to Maxwell crying, holding the pregnancy test in her hand. She kept looking at it, thinking it might change: she needed it to change.

"Jono, I'm sorry, but I have to address the elephant in the room." Jono looked at him, wiping her nose with her sweatshirt sleeve.

"I give, what's the elephant?"

"I need you to be honest with me. I need you to think about this. Was Mike the last person who you, you know…"

"Had sex with?" she snapped. "Yeah, I'm pretty sure I'd remember if he wasn't." She scoffed at the idea of having sex so soon after Mike. As much as she hated him, when she thought about the time they had together, she wasn't ready to let those memories be washed away by being with another man.

"I'm sorry, I had to ask," Maxwell smiled. Jono nodded.

"I know."

Maxwell patted her on the leg. He had no idea what to say next. Jono calmed down and stopped crying. Maxwell sat silently staring at the wall. Jono continued to stare at the stick. Maxwell finally broke the very awkward silence. "Can I get you something to eat?" He stood up from the couch.

"Yes please, I'm starving." They moved back into the kitchen. Jono sat at the table, and Maxwell started pulling out items to make them breakfast. Jono started to cry again, a much more emotional cry: this pain was coming from her heart. Maxwell set down the frying pan and went to her. He knelt on the floor in front of her. Jono collapsed in his arms, crying uncontrollably. "What do I do now?"

Jono and Maxwell talked all day and late into the night about her newly discovered condition. The reality of being pregnant was a great deal to absorb for Jono. The fact that it was Mike's forced her to think about him. She tried every day to not think about Mike, but he was always on her mind. That evening, while eating some Chinese food they had delivered, Jono got up to get a beer.

"What are you doing?" Maxwell asked politely.

"It's a beer? What's the matter, you want one?"

"Jono…" He pointed at her tummy.

"Oh shit! Right!" She put the beer back in the refrigerator. "Max, you have to help me," she told him as she sat back down. "I have no choice, right?" They'd already gone over this a hundred times.

"Jono, you always have a choice. The only question is, do *you* want to have this baby? Not having the baby means you never have to worry about seeing Mike, your career will not be affected - you know, life goes on. Of course, having the baby changes just about everything. Your career, if not over, will be put on hold for quite some time. You'll have no choice but to have some kind of contact with Mike and, well, I can't think of an 'and': those are the two most important things. Actually the 'and' is… do you want to be a mom? Are you ready for something like this? This is the real question you need to ask yourself." Maxwell felt good about how he explained her options. "I know this is not simple, and you know what else, this certainly is not something that has to be decided today."

"I know. You're right. A mom: wow, that's weird. Even saying it feels funny. I can't believe I have Mike's baby in me. This must be a fate thing: I'm being punished or something."

"Yeah, I don't think so. This baby is the by-product of sincere love. I have never truly seen you so happy as you were when you were with Mike." Jono looked at him; she was confused.

"Are you defending him? Are you defending what he did?" Jono started to remember and was starting to get angry.

"No, no. Nothing like that. And I'm not suggesting you have the baby. I'm just trying to get you to remember where the baby came from, that's all."

"Oh. You mean a back-stabbing gold-digger, then?"

"Uh, yeah. That's what I meant," Maxwell took in a deep breath. "Jono, we've been talking for hours, in all that time do you realize you only mentioned abortion one time?" Jono looked up at him. She put her hand on her stomach. Her face started to change, and her eyes welled up. "Oh, Jono, I'm so sorry." Maxwell pulled her to him. Jono lay across his chest and cried herself to sleep.

For the next couple of days, Jono's situation was the only thing they talked about. Maxwell was finally able to get Jono out of the house; they went out to eat, they went shopping, they did things that Jono loved to do. She completely stopped drinking, and Maxwell noticed she was eating much better than she had in a while. Jono seemed to be changing: she was calm, no yelling, no tantrums. On the very first outing they went to a favorite café. Maxwell could see the wait staff arguing in the back: he knew they were fighting over who *had to* take Jono's table; no one wanted to throw themselves into the mouth of the wolf. Yes, she was that bad.

Jono and Maxwell discussed the ramifications of the two options: one list was very long, the other very short. Maxwell was actually surprised Jono wasn't forcing him to set an appointment for her to make this 'problem' go away. *Is she seriously considering keeping the baby?* he asked himself. Maxwell was trying his hardest not to influence or sway her decision: it needed to be her decision and hers alone. But in his heart Maxwell was hoping Jono would keep the baby, even though he knew it would change everything; Jono's career would be, for the most part, over, and his career would be, for the most part, over, but strangely Maxwell was okay with that.

Then, late one evening while Maxwell was watching the television, Jono came out of her room to talk to him. Maxwell could tell she had been crying. Jono sat down next to him and put her head on his shoulder.

"I can't keep the baby," she whimpered. "I can't do it, Max." Maxwell lifted her head off his shoulder and sat her up. She was a mess. Her eyes were swollen and red, her beautiful, long hair was tangled and went everywhere, and she was pale and looked sickly.

"I'll support whatever you decide, you know that." Jono nodded. "Can I ask why?" Jono started to tear up again.

"Because it's Mike's." She had the saddest face Maxwell had ever seen.

"I understand. I'll look into making arrangements. Don't worry, honey, you'll be fine." He smiled. Jono lay back down on his shoulder.

The next couple of days were hard but better. Jono had made up her mind and she knew it was the right decision. Having a baby now would alter her career forever; she wasn't ready for that. Plus the baby would be Mike's, a constant reminder, a hurtful reminder that she didn't want to have. And the scariest part, if she kept the baby she knew she'd have to reach out to Mike. That she couldn't do.

On the day of the appointment, Jono was remarkably calm, almost jovial. Maxwell took it in his stride: he didn't know where her head was at, but he was ready for anything. They pulled up to the clinic, which was way out-of-town. A place that Maxwell had been to many times with other "friends". He pulled right up to the back door where two nurses were waiting. They walked up to Jono's side of the car and threw two big black blankets over her as she stepped out, completely covering her. They all hurried into the clinic through the back door.

No one else except the doctor was there. The clinic made special arrangements with Maxwell to open early for Jono. Jono was relieved. The clinic was beautiful, Jono thought. Pretty colors, relaxing music, not a hospital feeling at all. That helped keep Jono calm. One of the nurses escorted Jono and Maxwell to the front lobby to have them fill out some of the necessary paperwork. Maxwell filled out all of the forms, using a false name, of course. Jono was told she had to read the medical release and disclaimer forms, then she signed them.

As she read the many pages she started to become anxious. She stopped at one point and reached for Maxwell's hand. He looked up, saw her face and squeezed her hand back. "It'll be over before you know it. Don't worry, honey, everything be fine," he assured her. They both went back to the paperwork. Jono was disgusted by the post-procedure precautions page. *Experiencing a little bleeding for several days is normal.* "Oh, that's nice." Most of what she read she expected, but she still hated reading it. Maxwell presented the paperwork to the nurse. "Thank you. We're ready for you. Come on back." The nurse directed them to a door that led down a short hallway. The nurse went in first, then Maxwell, then Jono. The room looked pretty much like her gynecologist's office, except for the bright colors on the walls. "Good morning, I'm Doctor Tupa. I'll be doing your procedure today."

"Morning, doctor, thank you for seeing us today," Maxwell greeted him back.

"Morning," Jono said in a very low voice. She was starting to feel it, it was getting real. Her heart was speeding up, her breathing was getting quicker, she felt a little dizzy. "Miss, if I could just have you change into this? There is a bathroom right here," the nurse opened the bathroom door, and Jono went in. She took off all of her clothes and put on the flimsy white gown. She sat down on the toilet, questions racing through her mind. "Jono? Are you alright?" Maxwell called out. "Yes, sorry. I'll be right out."

Sixty seconds later, Jono was lying on the bed, her feet elevated in stirrups. Maxwell was at her head, holding her hand. Having him there was a clinic exception, but a necessary one. Jono was given a local anesthetic, tears began to roll down her cheeks. Maxwell wasn't looking, he turned his head away. The doctor rolled his stool right up to Jono, between her legs. The doctor told Jono to expect some pressure. She felt him touch the inside of her thigh: without warning, an instinctive reaction, Jono slammed her legs closed, crashing her knees into the doctor's head. Maxwell turned back. The doctor was on the floor.

"Jono, what did you do?" Maxwell went to the doctor. "Are you okay?" he asked. Maxwell and the nurses helped the doctor to his feet. Maxwell turned and saw that Jono was sitting up on the bed. "What are you doing?" he questioned.

"Maxwell, take me home." She stood up and walked to the doctor. "I'm so sorry," she told him with a huge smile on her face. "You're going to be a great mother," he smiled back. Jono quickly ran into the bathroom, threw on her clothes and raced Maxwell back to the car. In that instant Jono became a mom.

Jono was transformed. Her life suddenly had new meaning, new purpose. She ate healthily, she regularly exercised, she even managed to get Maxwell to go on walks with her. She was happy every minute of every day. She read every book she could get her hands on that had anything to do with having and raising a baby. She and Maxwell painted and decorated one of Jono's spare rooms, turning it into the perfect nursery.

"You know I can't read a crystal ball, but apparently you can," Maxwell laughed. "I'm assuming you think it's going to be a boy?" He smiled.

"No, Max. I know it's going to be a boy." Not only did they paint the room three shades of blue, but Jono purchased everything she could that signified boy: sports posters, a baseball glove, a football, and she even ordered a custom-made surfboard from Hawaii: the smallest surfboard she could get.

Maxwell and Jono discussed her future... their future, at length nearly every day. They came up with a plan, but for now they needed to keep Jono's substantial secret a secret. The biggest obstacle was when to announce, and how. It had to be soon: Jono was really starting to show. Jono and Maxwell agreed that they needed to let Mike know before Jono formally announced; this was important to Jono. They also decided not to announce until after the IMA, the International Model Award show held every year in New York. Jono was up for the top award and had already committed to being a presenter. The show was in two weeks: it was way too late and totally unprofessional to back out now.

Jono thought often about Mike and the fact that she was carrying his baby. She would put her hands on her tummy and think of him; she tried to think of the Mike she wanted to remember. She worried about how he would react, what he would say, what, if any, demands he would make. Maxwell advised they not seek a lawyer until after they spoke with Mike, not until they knew what his reaction was going to be. No matter how many fond memories she had of their time together, she always came back to the pain he caused her.

The dress Jono had made for her months ago for the awards show was no longer an option. When she tried it on, Maxwell burst out laughing. "I can't say out loud what you look like!" Jono looked in her full-length mirror: she couldn't help but laugh right along. Under normal circumstances, something like this would have set Jono over the edge, but as she looked at her belly sticking out of the beautiful chiffon dress it warmed her heart.

Getting a dress now, two weeks before for the big night, served to be a much larger challenge than Maxwell had thought. Normally he and Jono could pick any designer they wanted: there was no one who wouldn't want to be the one to make a dress for Jono, especially for this night. But every designer who was anything was already slammed with work trying to get all the last-minute orders out. Then Maxwell had an idea.

He called a friend who called a friend and got the number he was looking for. Funny, not one person asked Maxwell why he needed the number of the top maternity clothing designer in the country. Thankfully she was based out of Los Angeles. Maxwell got her on the phone right away. "Ms. Carlsen, again thank you for taking my call and for your discretion. We look forward to meeting with you." Maxwell hung up the phone and looked at Jono. "Well, that's set."

"This oughta be different." Jono smiled.

Early the next morning they were at Ms. Carlsen's studio. She greeted them at the back door to her shop. When Jackie Carlsen saw Jono, instinctively she looked down at her belly. Jono smiled. "Okay then, come on in," Jackie told them both. "This is a tall order, but I think I can put something together that you like," Jackie expressed promisingly. They got right to work, taking measurements, looking at fabrics, drawing up designs. For hours they worked on the dress design: it had to be at a high fashion level, it had to be striking, it had to be sexy, but it *had to* hide Jono's condition. Jono was being much more supportive than she would ever normally be in this kind of environment; she knew she was asking a lot. Six or seven hours later, they agreed on the dress design, material and color.

"Thank you so much, Jackie, I know it's going to be just beautiful."

"Not nearly as beautiful as the one who will be wearing it." Jackie smiled and hugged Jono. Right away they had a bond. "I will keep you posted, but expect a call for the first fitting in about a week," she told Jono and Maxwell. Maxwell kissed Jackie on the cheek.

"You're a life-saver."

"Not to worry, we'll get it done," she told him confidently.

THE IMA'S

The IMA is the crown jewel of the modeling world, and also for the fashion industry. Every top designer would be present, all with a dress or two being worn by some of the models. Jono was a wreck, but she was ready. She had her hair and make-up done in her hotel room by her staff. Jono wore a big, thick robe the whole time so as not to give her secret away. She trusted every single person on her staff but still, the less people who knew, the better, Maxwell convinced her. Their massive limo pulled up in front of the theater; there were hundreds of news reporters, fashion reporters, paparazzi and fans waiting in designated areas, all around the front of the building. Flashbulbs and lights, people screaming out names trying to get the attention of someone so they would look their way for a photograph.

"You ready?" Maxwell asked. Two tuxedoed security ushers were waiting to open the door. Jono took a deep breath.

"I've done this so many times, it's never bothered me. This time I feel like I could get sick any second," Jono told Maxwell.

"Well, if you decide you're going to get sick, please wait till you're talking to Jessie James (the outlaw of gossip reporters, her own title).

Jono started to laugh voraciously: it worked. Maxwell tapped on the window. One of the security guards opened the door. Jono got out first: the fans started screaming her name, the camera flashes were beyond a strobe light pace, but this was familiar territory for Jono. Jono's handler or escort came up and introduced herself to Jono and Maxwell. Her job was to make sure Jono stopped in all the right places and talked to all the right people as she worked the red carpet.

Jono looked down at her dress and pretended she was fluting it, even though she checked herself in the mirror a hundred times; even though Maxwell and Jackie both told her no one would be able to tell, Jono was worried. She walked the red carpet holding a small handbag right in front of her, instead of the usual position down to her side. She stopped many times to pose for the photographers, never dropping her purse or hands from her midriff area. She spoke to several television and magazine reporters. Her handler breezed by James, and Jono smiled graciously.

Once inside, Jono and Maxwell were stopped dozens of times by friends and acquaintances, all wanting to say hi or take a quick picture with Jono. Minutes later, the theater bells started ringing, letting everyone know the show was about to start and they needed to get to their seats. Jono and Maxwell where escorted the rest of the way to their seats, center front. They sat down; Jono moved in close to Maxwell.

"Do you think anyone could tell?" she whispered.

"No, I'm sure of it," he patted her hand. "Relax and enjoy the show, have fun." Jono nodded. She knew the red carpet was the appetizer, it was dark out, people all around, bright lights, all working in her favor. But in minutes she would be onstage where everyone would see her with no obstructions, with television cameras zooming in as close as possible. She was starting to get very antsy and started squirming in her seat. Thankfully the first break came up, and an usher came up to Jono and Maxwell. "We need you backstage now." They got up and followed him to a backstage waiting area.

Jono and Maxwell knew everyone who was waiting backstage; they quietly made the rounds greeting everyone. Jono's dress was the talk of the backstage area. "Jono, you look amazing, radiant even," one of her modeling friends told her. "And your dress, it's gorgeous... Who made it?" another other model asked. "Oh, kind of an unknown, I'll tell you about her later." Jono was being ushered into position just off-stage: she was up next. A stage manager stood right next to her, then came loud applause, then Jono was announced. "Now," the stage manager signaled to Jono.

Jono took a deep breath then walked out onto the giant stage with grace and poise. Enormous applause: she waved and smiled. Jono got to the podium and adjusted the microphone down a little. "Hey, everybody!" Jono was being Jono: the nerves were gone. She had the audience laughing and applauding the entire time she was out onstage. She announced the musical group that was coming up next; smiled, waved and walked off-stage. Maxwell waited right behind the curtain. He gave her a big hug. "The dress," Jono quietly yelped. Maxwell jumped back, she was kidding. It was almost as if Jono didn't care anymore. They went back to their seats and continued to enjoy the show.

The last award of the night was *the* award: the International Model of the Year Award. Jono had won the award one time before, but fully did not expect to win tonight, not with the year she had had. She was nominated but that didn't mean much, for the last several years it was usually her and the same four other top models who seemed always to be nominated. Each model was showcased on the big screen onstage with photographs set to music from different shoots from that year. Each of them had stunning photographs to represent them. Jono was not easily impressed, but she was.

Jono was the fourth one announced: her photographs were plastered on the massive screen and the other hundred televisions that wrapped around the theater. Jono watched and remembered each one, where she was, who she was modeling for, who was there, all of it. A photo from the Hawaii shoot was one of the first ones to come up; Jono's heart started to race. Without thinking about it she put her hand on her belly and smiled. But it was the second to last photograph that really stood out to Jono. She stared at it hard. Her memory of that shoot was vague, not like the rest. All at once Jono reacted. "Oh shit!" she said, way too loud. The audience around her thought she was just being funny, but she wasn't. Maxwell turned to her. "What's wrong?"

"Max, I need my phone," she demanded as quietly as she could.

"Why, they're just…"

"Max," she held out her hand. Maxwell handed her her phone. She opened up the photos and raced through them: she had every shoot in a different file. The last model was introduced and her photographs were on display.

"What are you doing?" Maxwell chided her. She didn't answer, she didn't look up. She was flipping through her thousands of photographs as fast as she could. She finally came to the shoot she was looking for: it was a shoot she had done early in the year in Mexico. She opened the file and started scanning through the photographs. She stopped cold on one of the photographs. *I knew it*, she said to herself.

"And this year's Top International Model is…" last year's top model announced as she opened the gold envelope, "…Jono!" The audience erupted. Everyone in the theater stood, clapping and calling out Jono's name. "Uh, Jono? Are you going to go get your award?" Maxwell asked her. Jono turned to Maxwell. "I won?" "Uh yeah, everyone's kinda waiting on you," he smiled. He took her arm and helped her to her feet. Jono looked up at the screen on the stage: there was her picture with her new title posted underneath.

But it wasn't winning that was on her mind. She was mad - no, she was scratch your eyes out pissed. She immediately snapped out of it, walked up the stage stairs, smiled, waved and acted as surprised as she could. She hugged last year's winner and excepted the mammoth trophy from her, which she immediately handed to one of the stagehands. Jono approached the microphone. She never took the time to prepare a speech, she'd had a lot going on and the last thing she expected was to win.

"Well, hi again!" she started. Everyone sat back down. "Let me start by thanking some very important people. Maxwell my manager, you all know Maxwell, right?" she yelled. Everyone applauded. Maxwell had no qualms about standing and taking a couple of bows. Jono went on to thank the rest of her staff, sincere in her words and tone. She thanked her fellow models whom Jono praised heavily. Then Jono broached a subject she didn't think she would.

"I know y'all have already seen me in my birthday suit but what do you think about this dress?" The audience erupted with laughter and applause. Maxwell was stunned but loved it. "This dress was made for me by a very dear friend, Ms. Jackie Tupa, you really need to check out her work." Everyone in the audience looked at each other: they had no idea who Jono was talking about. "Anyway, as you know, this has been a, well… let's be honest, crazy year for me. Whew!" She motioned as if she were wiping her forehead. "I've been all over the map and all over the globe!" The audience was soaking it up, laughing hard. "As you know… I died this year." Jono made a very serious face; the audience was unsure how to react, and it got really, really quite. Maxwell sat with his hand over his open mouth, afraid of where Jono was going with this. Jono smiled then laughed, it was almost like the audience had been holding their collective breath. They quickly followed with mild applause. "Yup. But I was saved by a very handsome fireman, he brought me back to life." Jono teared up a little. "Mike Johnson, you've probably heard his name once or twice." Everyone including Maxwell laughed. "So here's the thing." She paused. "I recently threw my hero under the bus, as deep and as hard as I could, but then I'm not telling you anything you don't already know," she joked. Then Jono stopped smiling and shifted into a very serious tone; she stood close to the mike and looked out at the audience. "I thought my hero, Mike Johnson, betrayed me; I thought this real and genuine man who made me laugh, cry and love my life…

was all a lie. He didn't hurt me, he loves me... but not as much as I love him." Tears were pouring down Jono's face and just about every woman's face in the audience. She had already gone way over her allotted time, but no one was going to cut her off. "I made a mistake, I was wrong. So I want to say to you," Jono motioned her hand from one side of the theater to the other, "and I want to tell Mike Johnson on national television... I'm sorry." Jono covered her face and ran backstage.

The audience were stunned. For many seconds they sat in total silence, then the music came on, snapping everyone out it. Every single person stood and gave Jono the loudest and longest standing ovation in recent memory. Maxwell ran up the front steps of the stage, ran right past the MC as he was wrapping up the show, and disappeared behind the curtains.

"I have no words," Maxwell said to Jono when he found her hiding in one of the dressing rooms. "I am truly speechless. However, I'd like to know what the hell just happened!" he barked. Jono was curled up in an oversized chair staring at her phone. She looked up at Maxwell, then handed him her phone.

"It wasn't Mike," she said with half a smile as she wiped away some tears from her face. Maxwell thought he understood but wasn't completely sure. He looked at the picture Jono had open on her phone.

"Are you talking about *the* pictures? The nudes that Mike sold?" he asked.

"Yes... No! That's what I'm trying to tell you..." Jono was tongue-tied and excited. "It wasn't Mike! Look closer... I realized as soon as I saw one of the pictures they were showing in the theater that the pictures that I thought Mike sold were actually from Mexico. Mike wasn't with me in Mexico!"

"Holy shit! Troy!"

"Exactly."

"I should have known..." Maxwell hesitated. "Jono, are you sure? This is a big deal, really big," Maxwell reminded her.

"One hundred percent. While they were showing my shoots from this year, when I saw this photo, I knew. I knew in an instant, it all came back to me. That asshole Troy took those pictures while I was, you know... not all together and used them to make money. That jerk... as soon as he knew his meal ticket was gone, he stabbed me in the back. Oh, man! It makes so much sense now," Jono stood up. "Maxwell, what have I done? The father of my unborn child thinks I hate him. I literally threw the perfect man to the wolves. I never gave him a chance."

Maxwell was trying to take it all in and put the new puzzle pieces together. "You're sure you're sure? I mean, this changes everything," Maxwell asked. Jono forced him to sit down, and she laid everything out step-by-step. She showed Maxwell the pictures from the shoot, then the naked ones that were posted on the internet. The details were subtle but they were there. "These *are* from Mexico!" Maxwell said excitedly. "It wasn't Mike, it was Troy!" He smiled at Jono. "Holy crap, what are we going to do now?" he asked.

Jono grabbed him by his hand. "Aren't there a few parties we are supposed to show our faces at?" she asked. Maxwell got it immediately.

"Yes, I believe there are." Jono got herself together then she and Maxwell walked out of the theater to the front of the building. There were reporters and fans everywhere. Limos were pulling up every other second. Jono was first approached by her nemesis, Jessie James, with lights, a camera and a microphone in her face. Jessie James was hated by nearly every person in the modeling world, none more so than Jono. She had put out some pretty nasty exposés on Jono, but right now she was glad Jessie was the first one to get to her. Maxwell moved in to block, but Jono waved him back, catching Jessie a little off guard. She didn't miss a beat. "Jono, congratulations on your award. That was quite a speech, I'm sure all of my fans would like to know what exactly is going on. What did you mean when you said your ex-boyfriend Mike was not the one who betrayed you? Can you explain?" Jono looked at Maxwell. He nodded his head then stepped back and let Jono go. At first Jono wasn't sure what she wanted to say and how much she should divulge, but as she spoke the words just came out, and she couldn't stop if she had wanted to. She held nothing back. She ripped into Troy, telling Jessie not only that it was Troy who sold the now famous photos, but she carefully touched on Troy's violent side. "What are you saying? Are you saying Troy has hit you before?"

"As a woman with experience, I feel it is my place, no, my responsibility, to warn other women about men such as him. I'm not saying anything about what happened between Troy and me, I'm simply putting out a warning, that's all." Jessie smiled: she knew she had a serious scoop. Then Jono changed her face and her tone; in a heartfelt and emotional way she apologized to Mike, begging for his forgiveness. Jessie stood there and listened: for the first time in her career she didn't have to ask any hard, probing questions. Jono laid it all out for her. When Jessie thought Jono was done, she looked at her. "Thank you," she said sincerely.

"Hold on, I'm not quite done." Jono stood tall, and Maxwell smiled. He was nervous, even scared, but he was proud of Jono. "Jessie, you're getting the scoops of scoops." Jessie looked like a junkie who had just taken a hit. "Okay, awesome." She looked at her cameraman who flipped back on the light, then he gave her the thumbs-up. "Go ahead," Jessie said.

"Well, I want everyone to know I'll be taking some time off, an extended vacation." Jessie looked disappointed by the announcement.

"Okay. I'm sure your fans will be disappointed but also understand." Jessie was about to cut the camera again.

"I hope so. I'm pregnant. And I'll need some time with my baby," Jono smiled. Maxwell was beaming like the proud uncle he would soon be. Jessie's mouth nearly hit the ground. Everyone who was within hearing distance turned their attention to Jono. Jono smiled and looked directly at Jessie.

"I couldn't be happier. Mike and I are very happy." That started a firestorm of questions from reporters who were mooching in on the interview. Jessie quickly moved into the logical questions. "When are you due? Do you know if it's a boy or a girl yet?" Jono had a newfound freedom, a confidence, an acceptance of herself. *I have to find Michael,* she thought to herself. As Jono wrapped up the interview, she proudly pulled her dress tight to her body to reveal the pooch around her tummy. The photographers went ballistic. Jessie was moved. "Congratulations," she told her excitedly. Maxwell grabbed Jono's arm. "Excuse me, ladies. Jono, we have a party to get to." Maxwell whisked her to the car where the rest of Jono's staff were waiting inside. Maxwell opened the door, Jono started to get in. Her staff gave her the stare down, cold faces and hard looks. Jono sat down. Maxwell got in and closed the door.

Jono started right in. "You guys, I am so sorry. I..." The car erupted with cheers and clapping, completely startling Jono. Everyone crawled over to Jono to congratulate her and give her a hug. "We are so happy for you," her make-up artist, Holly, told her. Jono was trying not to cry. "I can't believe it, you guys are so amazing. I love you all so much!" She tried again to apologize but no one would let her. Jono gave in, she understood her staff, she knew who they were, what kind of friends they had become. She hated herself for not treating them the way they had always treated her. Jono couldn't hold back the tears and neither could anyone else in the car. Soon afterwards, the car pulled up in front of a well-known New York hotel landmark. It looked as if the entire audience from the theater were all standing out in front. A long line of party guests wrapped around the building down the block as far as you could see. There was a red carpet for all to walk on, giving everyone a chance at the feeling, even if it was only for a hundred feet.

Jono, Maxwell and Jono's entourage got out of the car and gathered on the sidewalk in front of the hotel. "Should we go in?" one of her staff asked. "No not yet, I'm waiting for one more of our group to get here." They all looked around at each other: no one had any idea who Jono was talking about. Jono's hairdresser,

Monica, tapped Jono on the shoulder. "Look," she nodded toward the parking valet. A brand new - it didn't even have license plates yet - yellow Ferrari pulled up. The driver got out and was screaming demands to the unfortunate young valet. He was telling him in a very demeaning way exactly where and how to park his car. The Ferrari driver then walked to the passenger side of the car and opened the door; however, he didn't help his passenger, who was wearing a very short skirt, out of the car. He just stood there posing for photographers while she struggled on her own to get out. Jono smiled. "Troy."

Jono was so tempted to approach Troy right then, but she held herself together. *Not the right time.* Troy somehow managed to bypass the long line, but didn't miss the opportunity to walk the red carpet. With his blonde bombshell, wannabe model, Troy worked the line hard. Troy made every photographer take his picture even if they weren't interested. Jono stood well hidden from the reporters and paparazzi: she was blocked by her friends and had her head covered. "Finally!" Jono said. Everyone turned to see what Jono was talking about. Jessie James and her cameraman were quickly walking down the sidewalk toward them.

"This is our other party?" Holly asked.

"It is," Jono smiled as she got closer.

"Jono, I'm so sorry. The station wouldn't let me leave the theater until I uploaded what I had. You should be on every news station as we speak," she smiled. Maxwell was so surprised at Jono's deviance, but loved it.

"Good. Should we go in?" Jono asked the group. Jessie reached out and stopped Jono.

"Jono, they'll never let us upstairs, you know, the 'no reporters allowed' thing, especially me." Jono coyly smiled.

"Just turn on your camera and keep it rolling." Jessie did just that and followed closely behind. All at once everyone in Jono's entourage looked at each other; without hesitation they got out their own phones and turned on the cameras or recorders, even Maxwell. They didn't know what was coming, but they knew it was going to be big.

Jono skipped the red carpet, much to Maxwell's disappointment, and walked directly to the heavily guarded front door. When they approached the first guard, Jono stopped; she said nothing. The guard looked at her, then over her group. "How many?" Jono turned and looked at her party, then turned back to the security guard. "This many." The guard motioned his hand for the group to continue inside. No one, especially Jessie, said a word. *Wow!* Jessie said to herself. The group was escorted to the express elevator, which only went from the lobby to the top floor. The entire top floor was the hottest private nightclub in New York. Because of the size of the group, they had to split into two, Jono had Jessie go with her in case anyone tried to stop her. Maxwell stayed with the second group to make sure everyone made it. "I've tried a million times, but this will be the first time I've ever actually made it inside," Jessie told her fellow elevator passengers. Jono smiled.

Once the elevator doors opened, they entered the lavish lobby area. Jessie told her cameraman to keep the camera on and turn the light on only when necessary. The lobby area was the only other place some select reporters and photographers were allowed to be. Cameras immediately started blasting away. Jono *was* the belle of the ball, this evening's *It girl*: she let the photographers snap away for several minutes. She never approached the reporters; she waved, they were pissed. Jono headed to the large arch that was roped off and draped with heavy black and gold curtains. There were six very large, tuxedoed security guards and two hostesses. Jono walked to the entrance to the club slowly, making sure everyone knew she was heading in. Only one of the hostesses spoke up, "Good evening, Jono. Welcome and congratulations. We are all excited that you're here." Jono nodded, then the group, including Jessie and her cameraman, walked in. You could hear the reporters in the lobby loudly bitching about it, but no one was listening.

The party was raging. Lights flashing, music pounding, people dancing: the club was over-the-top impressive. It was a sea of who's who in the modeling world. Jono was spotted by the club's owner right away. "Jono!" He approached and gave her the one-cheek-two-cheek kiss, then he greeted Maxwell the same. "Welcome, welcome!" he announced. Then he spotted Jessie, and looked at Jono. "My crew," she told him. "Yes. Of course." Then he leaned into Jono. "You scared me, I wasn't sure you were coming. There are so many people who want to meet you," he told her. Jono shook her head. "Of course, anyone you want," she smiled supportively. "I have you at our best table, it's just up the stairs..." He looked at the size of the group, "Ah, I don't think we'll be able to sit everyone at your table. Would you like me to try to find something else?" But before Jono could speak up, her personal assistant Karen did. "I'm good! I'd rather dance and mingle anyway," she announced. Nearly half of the group agreed with Karen. Jono hugged everyone of them, thanked them, and then they agreed they would regroup in the lobby at midnight. Peter was relieved.

Jono, Maxwell, Jessie and the remaining associates were escorted by Peter past more security, up some iron stairs that ran up one entire side of the club to the second level. He took them to a large booth on the far side of the balcony. The private booth was surrounded on three sides by long, dark, black and gold curtains; it could be as private as you wanted it to be. It overlooked the entire first floor of the club. The view out of the windows was breathtaking: you could see the New York skyline for miles. Peter pulled back the curtain and secured it to the wall. "My best!" he said proudly to Jono. "Perfect, Peter, thank you." He nodded and bowed. "A dance later?" he shyly asked. "I'd be disappointed if we didn't!" The group sat, watched and drank their first round of drinks, provided to them by their host, Peter; Jono drank sparkling water. Jessie was amazed. Maxwell was bouncing in his seat: he needed to dance and it had better be soon. "What do you think, guys? Should we go dance?" Jono asked the group. That was all Maxwell needed: he sprang up from his seat and grabbed Jono's hand. Jono turned to Jessie. "Stay close." Jessie nodded. She and her cameraman were right behind.

Jono barely got one foot on the floor and the music suddenly got very quiet: everyone turned and looked at the DJ. "Ladies and gentlemen, it gives me great pleasure to announce to you... This year's Top International Model... JONO is in the house!" A bright spotlight shone down on Jono and her group. Jessie signaled to her cameraman to turn on his light and get some of the action. Everyone applauded and cheered. Jono curtsied to the DJ and waved to the crowd. Many partiers circled around Jono to congratulate her or just reach out to touch her; the music was cranked back up. Jono and Maxwell were dancing up a storm. Jono loved to dance with Maxwell, he was so animated. Many guys and a few women came up to try to cut in to dance with Jono, but she politely declined. "Maybe a little later," she told them; she wanted to get at least one full dance in with Maxwell. All of her entourage moved onto the dance floor and circled Jono and Maxwell; they ended up dancing together in one big group. Everyone was having a great time, especially Jono. Maxwell could see it on her face, for the next several songs she forgot about everything and just had fun. Or at least Maxwell thought.

The music shifted to a slow, quiet song. The group stopped dancing, but continued to mill around on the dance floor, talking and hanging out. A number of people came up to Jono to congratulate her; some requested a photo with the Model of the Year, and Jono gracefully obliged. It was Holly who first spotted the incoming trouble: she gave Jono a heads-up. Jono glanced over at Jessie: she was ready.

"Jono!" There came a loud, painful to hear, familiar voice. There stood Troy, grinning from ear to ear, his date standing five feet behind him. Jono slowly turned to face him. "Troy," she acknowledged in a low tone and with the thinnest smile. Maxwell moved as close as he could to Jono. "Maxwell," Troy said, acknowledging his presence. Maxwell didn't respond. Speaking very loudly as if he were making an announcement, he said, "I wanted to congratulate you on your well-deserved award. I think it's amazing! You so deserve it!" Then he started to step closer, moving in to hug Jono or perhaps attempt to kiss her, it didn't matter. Jono stepped back, defeating Troy's approach. He laughed.

"Why do you have to be like that?" he jested. "Aren't we friends?" he asked, dripping with sarcasm. Jono's expression did not change.

"Speaking of friends, who is that you're hiding behind you?" Jono asked.

"Oh," Troy turned and looked back at his date. "That's my date, Lori." He didn't try to bring her into the conversation; he didn't even introduce Lori to Jono. Jono had had enough.

"Anything else?" Jono asked, gritting her teeth. Troy looked a little confused, almost flustered; he wasn't sure how to respond. Jono took a half-step to one side so she could see Lori. "How long have you and Troy been dating, Lori?" Lori smiled.

"Oh, this is our first date… but it hasn't been going so well," she shyly admitted. Troy was getting red; his face was tight, and several veins on his forehead were protruding. Jono recognized this look. Maxwell was doing everything he could to keep himself from losing his cool.

"Lori, I don't know you, but please, for the sake of all women, never ever take your clothes off around this guy." Everyone who heard the remark either covered their faces so as not to show their smiles, or, in Maxwell's case, outwardly laughed. You could see it: Troy's head was spinning, not exactly what his little ego expected. Troy started to turn, and he reached out to take Lori's hand. She refused him. "So Troy?" Troy stopped and turned back, now beet-red. "What?" he snapped. "I was just wondering how much money you got for my nude photos?" Jono was smiling. Troy advanced toward Jono very quickly, with his finger as his weapon yelling at the top of his lungs.

"That's none of your business, bitch!"

Jono took one step back and with her skinny arms, but big hands, clocked him right in the jaw! Troy went down like Jell-O. The hundred people who were right there in the mix of the whole thing started applauding, even Lori. Jono was shaking her hand to fight off the pain, but it was worth it; she looked over at Jessie who was smiling from ear to ear, then gave Jono a thumbs-up. Security came running up to the growing crowd. "What happened?" Troy was starting to come to. "I've got it all right here," Jessie told the security.

"Maxwell... I think it's time for us to go." Maxwell's smile was glued to his face.

"I believe this party has become boring," he laughed. "Where to?"

"Hawaii!"

"Of course!"

VACATION WITH A CATCH

Very early the next morning, Jono, Maxwell, and Jono's entire entourage were on-board a jumbo jet headed for Hawaii. It was a crazy twenty-four hours, to say the least. Jono had Maxwell put everyone in one coach so they could all be together, including her and Maxwell. Her whole staff, and most of the world, now knew Jono's story. Everything Jono had done up to now was easy: the hard part was yet to come. She knew she had crushed Mike, maybe hurt him beyond repair. But she knew she had to talk to him, she had to try her best to explain… She had to let Mike know he was about to be a dad again.

One of Jono's staff was watching the news on his computer. "Hey, Jono! Come over here, you're going to want to see this," he smiled. She sat down next to him. "What's up?" she asked. "Morning news," he answered. They and as many as could get close enough watched intently. "Some of you may not have been up late enough to see this amazing video that came out of one of the after-parties after the IMA last night. You're not going to believe it." The news announcer paused. 'A video on loan from Jessie James' popped up on the screen: Jono smiled. The video first showed a few seconds of Jono

163

dancing with Maxwell, then it cut to her confrontation with Troy. You could hear all the dialog perfectly. Jono was blasting Troy, then the punch - down goes Troy! Everyone on the plane applauded. Jono and Maxwell were laughing hysterically. Jono started to get up. "Hold on, Jono, there's more," her staffer told her. "More?" Jono sat back down.

Apparently Jessie kept recording after Jono had left. The video showed two oversized security guards helping Troy get up. Troy dusted himself off, said a few choice words that all had to be bleeped out, then one of the guards took him by the arm to escort Troy out of the party. Troy turned and swung on the guard as hard as he could. The guard gnarled at him, then the video stopped. The news anchor was outwardly laughing. "What was that guy thinking?" he chuckled. "And now onto more news."

"Oh my God." Jono put her hand up to her mouth. She looked around at her staff, then Maxwell, everyone was waiting to see Jono's reaction. She stood up and dropped her hand: she was smiling as widely as her face would allow. She looked around the plane then loudly burst out, "Champagne for everyone!" Everyone on-board clapped and cheered. The flight crew couldn't help but clap with everyone else. Minutes later, champagne was flowing to every single passenger, of age, on the plane.

Jono sat back down next to Maxwell. "That was fun," Maxwell told her as he sipped his champagne.

"It was." The excitement and smile left Jono's face. Maxwell didn't have to ask, he knew.

"Jono, everything will be alright… I'm sure of it," he said to her. Jono looked at him with big, sad eyes.

"I'm such an idiot, I hate myself right now. How could I…?" She was interrupted by Maxwell.

"It is what it is, Jono. You need to forgive yourself so you can move on. You've admitted your mistake and now you're trying your best to rectify it. Let it go… these things have a way of working themselves out. This will, too," Maxwell explained to her.

"But what if it's not okay? What if he refuses to even see me? I know he hates me: he must hate me. He's going to hate me even more when he finds out I'm carrying his baby," she said, terrified.

"You don't know that." Maxwell tried his best to console her. "We've been over this a hundred times already, Jono. If the worst happens, if for some reason Mike, you know, just doesn't want anything to do with us, then you and I will take a nice, long break, go somewhere amazing, you'll have the baby and we'll make decisions after that, right?" He reached over and lifted her chin off her chest.

"Right." Jono took a huge, deep breath and gathered her thoughts. "So, were you able to get a hold of Kaleen or Kale?" she asked.

"No, not by the time we took off. You know it was two in the morning in Hawaii, but I'll call the second we land."

"But they know we're coming?"

"Yes, that's all been taken care of."

"Okay, good. They must know where Mike is. If they haven't talked to him I'm sure they've seen him?" she questioned.

"I'm sure you're right. We'll know soon enough: only about an hour to go." Maxwell smiled as he reached out to hold her hand. It was one of the longest hours of Jono's life. Jono sat quietly holding her tummy, thinking. Everything she said, everything she did to Mike, made her angry at herself. *I didn't give him a chance, I didn't even give him the opportunity to defend himself. I'm such an idiot.* Jono was a bundle of nerves: she was scared yet excited. She wanted to see Mike so badly, but she was convinced the damage was so great that *they* didn't have a chance. She was holding onto the hope that Mike would at least be excited about being a father again. *He has to, he just has to,* she thought. She spent the remainder of the flight role-playing in her mind what she would say when she saw him. *How am I ever going to explain my actions? How do I tell him about the baby?* None of her ideas ended well.

To no one's surprise, there were hundreds of reporters waiting for Jono as she exited the airport. Jono decided it was best to meet them head-on. She smiled and waved, she even pulled her sweatshirt tightly to her body so everyone could see her swollen tummy and get a picture. The reporters were eating it up. Jono didn't want to answer any questions, but Maxwell thought it would be a good idea to answer a few. "Jono, did you hear what happened to Troy?" was a question that caught her attention.

"I did, just a few minutes ago," she smiled.

"Do you have any comment?" the same reporter asked. Jono thought for a second before she spoke.

"I think Troy needs some help, and I think now he'll get what he needs." She wanted to say so much more, but she resisted. She knew if she came at him again it would only make her look petty and this time it would be bad press.

"Have you spoken to Mike Johnson?" one of the reporters asked. Jono wasn't sure how much the reporters knew. She decided it would be best to play it safe. The last thing she wanted was to take a chance that Mike might see her being followed by a bunch of reporters while she looked for him, and admitting that she didn't know where he was would only create more questions.

"Yes. We are in constant contact..." Maxwell cut her off.

"Sorry, guys, we've got friends and family waiting on us. Plus we don't want Momma standing on her feet too long." He smiled. The reporters all smiled and laughed in support.

Jono wanted to try to keep their presence in Hawaii as low-profile as possible, but she knew that was not going to happen and she would have to appease the reporters, otherwise they would be on her like glue, no matter how hard she might try to hide. So, to start with, she had Maxwell order three passenger vans instead of the usual limousines. Jono knew reporters would be everywhere, lurking, waiting to capture that one shot: she wanted to do everything possible to prevent it. She had Maxwell schedule an interview or shoot of sorts on Waikiki Beach, which is a fair distance from Dan's house. Maxwell told the reporters to expect Jono to pose in a bikini. That got everyone's attention. Then Maxwell made lunch and dinner reservations for the next few days at several restaurants all over town in hopes of distracting and splitting up as many of the paparazzi as possible. Jono's staff would split up into three groups: they would each go to a different restaurant and only decide on the restaurant at the last minute. To keep up the rouse, Jono planned to go a few times so she would be spotted. The idea, they hoped, would give Jono and Maxwell unmolested time to find and hopefully talk to Mike.

"Did you get a hold of Kaleen?" Jono anxiously asked the second the van door closed.

"Yes, she's ready for us." Maxwell paused. "I'm sorry, Jono, Kaleen said they haven't seen or talked to Mike in over three weeks." Jono looked completely dejected. "Don't worry, honey, if he's on this island we'll find him." Jono tried to smile.

Kaleen and Kale were waiting in front of Dan's house as the three vans pulled in. Kaleen was waving like crazy with excitement. "Aloha! Aloha!" she greeted each person as they got out of the van, putting beautiful leis around their necks as she did. "Only Kaleen!" Jono smiled. Kaleen turned her attention to Jono. "Jono! I am so happy to see you. I'm so glad you're back. Kale and I have missed you terribly!" Jono was beaming.

"Thank you, it's good to be back," Jono said sincerely. She was amazed at how much she had missed the smells, the sounds, the tropical breeze. But her stomach was aching badly, not because of the baby, but because of the hole she had created. She missed Mike: all of the memories came crashing in like a large ocean wave. Kaleen held a large white and red lei in her hand, presenting it to Jono. "This one is for you," she told her. "You and the baby." She smiled.

"Kaleen, it's so beautiful. You really shouldn't have." Jono bent over to receive the lei. "It smells like Heaven." Kaleen kissed her face and then shocked Jono by kneeling on the ground in front of her. Kaleen put her face very close to Jono's stomach and quietly whispered a Hawaiian prayer to the unborn baby. Jono started to cry.

Maxwell stepped over. "That has to be special." He helped Kaleen to her feet. Kaleen smiled at Jono. "Thank you." Jono didn't know what to say. "You're welcome."

"Come on, let's get everyone inside and settled!" Kale announced. They were twelve in total, counting Jono and Maxwell. Kaleen had everything set up and organized. Jono and Maxwell each got their own rooms; the remaining staff were split up into two's and took the remaining four bedrooms and one of the dens. It was perfect: plenty of space and plenty of bathrooms. Everyone dropped their bags as they entered the house, amazed and in awe. Kale had the glass sliding walls tucked away, leaving the house open to the deck, the sand and the sea. Jono started laughing when she saw the faces and heard some of the comments. Everyone migrated to the deck. Two of her staff ran for the beach without missing a beat. Jono sat at one of the tables on the deck, and Maxwell sat down next to her. "Jono, this is great, really great," he told her.

"Waaaay overdue." Jono smiled. She had a such a somber look on her face; Maxwell knew it was hard for Jono to enjoy where she was right now. "Here we go," Kaleen declared as she and Kale approached the group with trays of food and drinks. Maxwell jumped to his feet to help out. Everyone excitedly gorged on Kaleen's fabulous treats, fresh fruits and tea. "Tea for you, Jono?"

"Oh, yes please."

"This will be very good for the baby," Kaleen told her while pouring her a glass.

"Kaleen, do you think you could sit with me for a minute?"

"Of course." Kaleen sat down and poured herself a glass of tea. "You want to ask me about Mike." Jono nodded. "I do." Kaleen tried to keep as positive a look on her face as she could.

"From the minute we watched you accept your award we have been looking everywhere and asking everyone about Mike. Kale even drove to the other side of the island." Jono's face was hanging as low as it possibly could; she started to whimper. Kaleen moved her chair as close to her as possible. She reached out and pulled Jono to her; Jono put her head on Kaleen's shoulder and started to cry.

"I am such a bad person... I've done so many bad things," Jono implored. Kaleen lifted her head, then wiped her tears with a napkin.

"Jono... you are not a bad person; you're sweet and kind, and generous. This I can tell you. I know you're going to be a great mother." Jono smiled then kissed Kaleen on the cheek.

"Thank you, I needed that." Jono sat back in her chair. "Do you have any ideas where I should look or maybe who I should talk to?" Jono asked as Maxwell came back and sat down.

"Well, Kale had some suggestions. They're not pleasant but I think it's important to rule everything out."

"What's that?" Maxwell jumped in.

"We need to contact the police to see if he's been arrested anytime recently and then, well, we need to contact the hospitals... just to make sure." Jono and Maxwell both nodded in agreement.

"On it!" Maxwell told them. "Holly!" he yelled out toward the beach. She looked up. "Yeah?" "Round up the troops, there's no time for play right now." "Okay!" Kaleen went in the house and got Kale and a phone book. Everyone came to the table. Kale was making suggestions and Kaleen was taking notes.

"Unfortunately we can't just call each of these places. If Mike managed to get arrested, it's likely he didn't use his real name. We have to go and show them photos." Maxwell was ready, he jumped up and went to his computer bag, then quickly came back with a handful of photos of Mike. "Nice," Kale smiled. Jono didn't think this far ahead; she was happy and impressed. "It's already getting late today, so let's start with these here." Kale pointed at the list. "These are the closest ones: it's a good start," Kale explained.

Jono was so happy. She was overwhelmed that all of these people were helping her. This was Jono's problem, but every person there made it feel like it was all of their problem. It was a lot to take in, but Jono didn't have time to be emotional anymore. Maxwell broke them into four teams: using the three vans plus Kale's truck, they could cover a lot more ground. Kaleen, Holly and Barbara went with Jono; Maxwell took three with him; the other van had four; and Kale took two. They decided on who got which police stations and hospitals and took off. When they reached the main security gates for the community, the paparazzi didn't know what to do. They started snapping pictures but they had no idea which vehicle Jono was in: it was useless to try to follow them. Their faces were priceless: everyone in Jono's van had a good laugh.

Jono's van got to their destination first. They pulled right to the front of the police station, and all four jumped out. Jono was still in her sweatshirt and pants; she rolled up her hair and hid it under a hat, trying to reduce the chances of being recognized. They went directly to the front desk. "Can I help you, ladies?" the police officer asked very politely. "Yes please," Jono spoke for the group. "We're looking for a friend. No one's seen him in about a month. We were wondering if maybe someone here has seen him, or maybe he might have been arrested?" she asked.

She handed the officer the photo. He looked at it closely. "This is Mike Johnson, right?" he asked to the surprise of the group. Maybe they got lucky on their first try. Jono got so excited.

"Yes! Yes it is! Do you know where he is? Is he here?" she desperately asked the officer. Jono was hopping up and down.

"I'm sorry, I didn't mean to mislead you, I only thought it was him because I've seen him on the television so many times. No, I'm sorry, he's not here. As far as I know, he's never been through here." Jono's emotions went from a ten to a one in a heartbeat. "You know what I'll do, though, I'll make sure all of the guys out of here know you're looking for him. We'll keep a watch out."

Jono was so dejected she was already walking for the door. "Thank you so much, officer. Here's my number if you hear anything." Kaleen handed him a piece of paper with her number.

"No problem. I promise, I'll let everyone know." Kaleen started for the door, "Excuse me?" The officer called out.

Kaleen turned back. "Yes?"

"Was that Jono?" the officer smiled.

"Yes."

Kaleen got in the van and crossed the station off the list. She contacted the other groups to see how they were doing. No one had anything to report; however, Maxwell had some good news. He had had the same experience at the police station they went to: everyone knew who Mike was but hadn't seen him. So Maxwell asked if it would be possible to ask the other stations - since everyone already knew what he looked like - if it was possible to ask around to see if anyone had seen him; or if not, would they keep a look out for him? "Brilliant!" Jono yelled over the speakerphone. It's always a good day when Jono calls you brilliant! So now everyone could concentrate on just the hospitals. After several hours of searching, not a soul had seen him. Maxwell called it, and everyone started heading for home. Jono was on the phone with Maxwell. "Jono, I promise, we'll get an early start tomorrow, we won't give up until we find him." "Thank you, Max... I love you, you know." "Yes, honey, I know."

Jono planted herself on the beach, close to the water. She sipped on some sparkling water while everyone else was trying every tropical drink known to man. They started a big bonfire; with some help, Kale moved the grill down to the beach. There was a ton of amazing food, especially Kaleen's special fish dish, Jono's favorite. Kaleen prepared a plate for Jono and herself, and went and sat down next to Jono. Maxwell and Kale followed right behind. While the 'kids' played they talked.

"Maybe Mike doesn't want to be found," Jono stated. "You know, we really don't even know if he's here. I just assumed this is where he'd be."

"He could have gone back to Denver?" Maxwell suggested. Jono nodded.

"No, I don't think so," Kaleen started. "There's too much here, too many memories. He'd never be able to leave."

"Maybe it's those memories that drove him away?" Jono said. Even Kaleen thought that could be true.

"I don't think so either." Maxwell spoke up.

"Why?" Kale asked.

"It's not just the memories for Mike. I know he loves it here, but it's more like he's emotionally connected. You know what I mean?" Maxwell asked, not sure if he sounded corny.

Jono stayed up late. She sat on the deck staring at the moon, the stars and the water: "glass-off". She smiled. She hoped she might get lucky and Mike would 'just show up' to his favorite surfing spot. When her eyes couldn't stay open a minute longer she went to bed, but still barely slept. The smell of bacon woke everyone up early, that and the food bell. Jono wanted to get as early a start as possible. This time they would be driving much further out. While eating breakfast, Kale came up to Jono and Maxwell. "I've been thinking about it," he started. "While we are all out covering the hospitals and such, maybe when we pass a beach where there are bums we should stop and show Mike's picture around. You never know. Aren't they the ones most likely to have seen him anyway?" he asked. Jono jumped up and gave Kale a big hug and kiss.

"Brilliant!" she told him.

"Why didn't I think of that?" Maxwell said, getting upset at himself. Jono had renewed energy.

They decided that two of the crews would go to the remaining hospitals while the other crews would hit the beaches. Jono was very excited. The two beach crews headed out in opposite directions with strict instructions that, no matter how small the hit, everyone else needed to be informed right away. It was a hot day, and Jono had to stop many times. Everyone was pounding water, trying to stay hydrated. They combed every beach they came to; they spoke to every bum they came across. None of them had seen Mike; only one even thought they recognized him. Exhausted, they had to take a break.

"Let's go back and rest. It's not good for you to be out in this heat," Maxwell suggested. "Besides, I think we might have better luck after dark."

"That's a good idea. Let everyone else know, please."

That night and the next day no one had any takers, not one. Jono started to feel really guilty. She dragged her crew all the way to Hawaii, only to sweat their asses off all day, for her? *How selfish can I be?* she taunted herself. She called Maxwell on his cell. "We're done. Have everyone meet back at the house, okay?"

"A break?" he asked.

"No. We're done," she told him. Maxwell could hear it in Jono's voice: she was exhausted and disappointed.

Back at the house, Jono sat on the couch with a cold compress on her head and a glass of tea in her hand. Eventually everyone got back. They all came in and sat around the living room. Kaleen was busy passing out tea. Jono's guilt grew even more when she saw all of the red and exhausted faces.

"Guys... I am so sorry. I owe you all an apology, I had no idea what I was dragging you into. I feel terrible. I'm not even sure Mike is actually here anymore." Many of her staff responded by telling her it was okay, they wanted to help, all things that Jono knew but couldn't have them be a part of a minute longer. "So listen, we are here for three more days; no more searching, no more talking to every bum we come across." Everyone laughed. "I want you to take the rest of your time in this amazing place and have a blast," she smiled. Jono fully expected a different reaction to the one she got. She thought they would be overjoyed, excited or happy at least. No clapping, no yelling with excitement. Barbara spoke up for the group. "Jono, we're here for you," she explained. "We will keep looking, we want to help.

Besides, I don't know about everyone else, but I'm having fun!" She smiled. *Now* everyone else cheered and clapped.

"You guys… I have no words. I'll tell you what, let's do this… We'll take tomorrow off: there are some places I have to show you, then we can decide after that what we should do. Is that a deal?" Everyone happily agreed.

The next morning after breakfast they all piled into two of the vans: Maxwell drove one, Kale drove the other. Jono had already told Kale and Kaleen the places and things she wanted everyone to see, so Kale had a route all worked out. They spent an amazing day seeing the sights. They swam, stood under a waterfall, saw Pearl Harbor, and ate a raw coconut - a highlight for Maxwell. Then they all went to a small restaurant that overlooked Waikiki Beach for dinner. Jono knew the sunset from there was fantastic, and she wanted everyone to experience it.

Maxwell let some of the paparazzi and reporters know that's where they'd be. He knew telling a few meant they would all know within minutes. Maxwell was not let down. There were too many bodies to count, all trying to get a picture, all yelling out questions. "Good idea," Jono told Maxwell. "Thanks!" he smiled. Jono posed, flashed her belly, but answered no questions. Nearly everyone had the same question: "Where's Mike?"

They group entered the restaurant. The owner meet them in the small waiting area. The restaurant had barely any walls, nearly every side was open to the water. "Beautiful!" was the overall response to the view. "Oh, and trust me the food is every bit as good!" the restaurant owner expressed. The small restaurant was empty, Maxwell arranged to reserve it only for only them so they could have as much privacy as possible and so they could be as loud as possible. Maxwell let one photographer in so he could take pictures of the night for everyone to have as a souvenir later.

The food was as the owner proclaimed, but the sunset was awe-inspiring. Everyone quickly took a group shot in front of the rail that separated the restaurant from the water, then they each grabbed their own phones and started snapping pictures of each other. Jono sat and watched. She was getting so much joy out of everyone having so much fun. Kaleen put her hand on Jono's; Jono turned to look at her. "This is such a good idea, these kids will never forget this," she told her. Jono smiled.

"I had to turn something bad into something good," she explained.

"Seems to me that's become your style lately." Kaleen rubbed Jono's tummy. Jono put her hand over Kaleen's. "Thank you."

HIDDEN TREASURE

For the next two days they would spend several hours a day looking under every rock and bush, and talked to as many people as they came across. Jono made sure, though, that every day also included as much fun as possible. Jono arranged for scuba lessons, surfing lessons and had four Sea-Doos anchored in the water out in front of the house for anyone to use. Jono wanted to surf so badly, but she knew she couldn't. So she lived vicariously through everyone else. For Jono it was an amazing amount of fun and laughs just to watch, especially Maxwell. Everything he tried he was a disaster at. Maxwell was a pretty big, pretty strong and seemingly athletic guy, but he had zero athleticism. Although Jono was confident, a lot of his mishaps in the water were on purpose to entertain her.

That night, Jono found herself walking the beach for miles by herself, thinking. It was calming, walking along in the light of the moon, the water rolling over her feet. She only thought about Mike. She thought and thought about where he might be. *He doesn't even know he's a dad. I even failed at that.* Jono said to herself. *What do I do now?* She decided she didn't know how or where, but she wasn't going to give up: she had to find him.

When they got back to LA, Jono was going to have Maxwell hire a private detective; she didn't care how much it would cost or how long it would take: this was something she had to do. She resolved to herself that even if she lost Mike, she wasn't going to let her baby not know his father. Kaleen told Jono it was a boy: now she knew she was right.

The last day no one went out looking: everyone reached the place Jono had reached days earlier. Instead they swam and played all day. But there was no way Jono was going to let the last night in Hawaii be like any other. With Kaleen and Kale's help - she didn't even want Maxwell to know - she planned a big beach party, but not just any kind of party, a luau! Toward the end of the day, Jono arranged for Maxwell and Kale to take the crew out to Diamond Head to see the inside of the dormant volcano and watch the sunset. They wouldn't be back till well after dark. Maxwell insisted he should stay, but Jono wouldn't have it. She played up the *I'm just going to eat and go to bed* line.

Minutes later, truck after truck were pulling up to the house. "Wow!" Jono smiled at Kaleen. Many men unloaded the trucks and moved everything to the beach. They set up a bamboo stage, with the front facing the back of the house; they set up tables and chairs, Tiki torches and serving stations. And they did it all very fast. But the best part was the pig. Two big, heavily tattooed men wearing grass skirts dug a large hole in the sand, put in some wood and lava rocks, then set it ablaze. "What's this?" Jono asked Kale. "Dinner," he joked. To Jono's amazement they set the pig inside, then completely buried it. Normally, to prepare a pig this way takes hours and hours. Kaleen used her influence to 'borrow' a pig from another luau that was already cooked.

Jono stood on the deck and looked over the beach, it was amazing, right out of a movie, she thought. Kaleen yelled out to Jono, "They're here!" Jono ran to the front door and went out front with Kaleen and Kale to meet the group. They all piled out of the vans with big smiles on their faces and bags of souvenirs under their arms. Jono stood in front of the door blocking anyone from going in. "What's going on?" Maxwell asked.

"Well, guys… this is our last night, I wanted to make it extra special. So with Kaleen and Kale's help we put together a little party for you." Before anyone could say anything or react, Jono clapped her hands. Four Hawaiian men came from around the corner of the house beating on Hawaiian drums, singing and dancing a native song. Everyone gasped and stepped back. Then the front door opened, four Hawaiian young ladies emerged from the house dancing in beautiful Hawaiian dresses and headdresses. Each of the dancers had armfuls of colorful leis. They walked up to each person and put several leis over their heads, then greeted them: "Aloha." Jono watched with great satisfaction. Then the drummers started nudging the group forward into the house. Some were lucky enough to be escorted by the lady dancers. They danced their way through the house, onto the deck, down to the beach, and on to the party.

Surrounded by Tiki torches, food and a bar, everyone was blown away. The music started. The dancers moved onto the stage and danced, sang and stomped to everyone's delight. When they were done, the music changed to a much quieter, beautiful Hawaiian song. Everyone came up to Jono to thank her; Jono just smiled. She was getting so much out of this. Maxwell already had a tropical drink with several small, brightly colored umbrellas sticking out of it when he walked up to Jono.

"You, my darling, have rendered me speechless." He stepped up to her and gave her a long hug, trying his best not to spill his drink on her. Jono looked at him with her coy little smile. "Mahalo."

They ate roasted pig, drank fruity drinks, sang and danced. Maxwell and a few others were even coaxed onto the stage to try their hand at the hula. Maxwell was surprisingly good. After the feast, dessert was served: no one had any room for it, but when they saw it was Kaleen's dessert they ate it anyway. Then a beautiful young Hawaiian girl stood center stage: Jono knew this was coming. "If I could ask everyone to follow me to the beach, please, for a special ceremony." Everyone looked at each other with the "What's going on now?" look, but got up and moved to the water.

The four Hawaiian men and four women were standing knee-high in the water. The young woman walked into the water holding Jono's hand who had already dropped her dress on the beach to reveal a bikini she was wearing underneath. "What's this?" Maxwell asked Kaleen. "You'll see." All nine of the Hawaiian performers, Kaleen and Kale started to sing. It was a Hawaiian blessing song for pregnant women, asking the gods of the sea and sky to bless the mother and the unborn child. The young woman knelt down in the water, and Jono followed. They all held hands and finished the song. Jono stood up, hugged each performer and walked out of the water to roaring applause and whistles from her friends. Each of her staff stood in a makeshift line so they could hug and thank Jono. It was not just beautiful, it was powerful.

Later that night after everyone had gone to bed, Jono found herself standing on the deck looking out over the calm water. She decided to take one last walk on the beach. She walked for some distance, playing with the waves as she walked. She thought about the day, how much fun everyone had had, how much fun she had had. Then she felt her stomach jump, starling her. *Whew, just gas!* she laughed at herself. It was late, it had to be two in the morning; they had an early flight so Jono started back.

She got back to the beach in front of the house. She turned and started to walk toward the house. Something startled her: she stopped and turned around. She looked at the ocean, then each way down the beach. She was all alone. She turned back and started walking. "I heard you were looking for me?" a male voice broke the silence. Jono froze. She didn't want to turn, maybe she was dreaming, but what if she wasn't. She quickly turned to face the voice. A tall, dark, muscular man was walking out of the water. He glistened in the moon. He looked big and powerful. Jono stood speechless. She fell to her knees and started to cry, putting her hands over her face. She couldn't face him: she thought she could, but she couldn't. Water dripped on her head. Mike was standing right over her. Her body trembled, but not from fear. "You came a long way," Mike spoke softly. Jono's mind was racing, *What do I say? What can I say?* Everything she'd thought about, every scenario she played out in her head vanished.

She continued sobbing, she didn't move, she didn't lift her head. "Jono." Jono looked up, Mike's hand was out: she took it. He helped her to her feet; her towel fell to the sand. Jono looked him straight in his big, brown eyes. She couldn't believe it: here he was, standing right in front of her. She started to step forward, but he quickly stepped back. "Oh! Oh, I'm so sorry. I'm sorry." She lowered her head in shame.

"Jono, why are you here?" Mike asked, letting go of her hand. She looked up, tears building in her eyes.

"I had to see you."

"Why?" Mike didn't raise or lower his voice, but was steadfast in his question.

"I have to… apologize, I have to tell you how sorry I am. I made an awful mistake." Tears started down her face. Mike stared at her. "I know it wasn't you, I knew it could be you!" she said angrily. "I… I'm so stupid. I have no excuse, what I did to you was evil." She shook her head in disgust. She reached down and picked up her towel, then wiped her face and nose. She smiled. "Sorry, same ol' girl." For the first time Mike smiled.

"I see that."

Jono started to calm down a little. She knew she needed to say what she had come to say. "Can we sit down?" she asked. She spread out her towel and sat on one side of it. Mike stood. "Oh." Jono stood back up. "Mike, I know what I did… was awful. I know there is nothing I can say that will convince you to forgive me. I didn't come here for that. I came to see you because I wanted you to know how sorry I am, and… and…" She lowered her head and started to cry much harder. She couldn't get the words out. She felt hurt and ashamed, embarrassed and humiliated. She knew she did this to herself, but she had to suck it up, she had to tell him.

"Is that my son?" Mike asked pointing at Jono's stomach. Jono's head sprung back up. She looked at him: he didn't look mad or upset, he looked… happy. Jono looked down at her stomach, then looked back up at Mike.

"Yes."

Mike stepped forward, stood right in front of Jono. Jono wasn't sure what to do or say; she didn't know what Mike was going to do or say, then he suddenly dropped to his knees. He reached around Jono's back and pulled her right to him. He slowly and gently kissed her stomach. Jono got chills all over her body. Mike whispered to her stomach: she couldn't understand what he was saying. Jono looked down at the back of Mike's head. She wanted to touch him so badly, she moved her hands behind her back. "What are you saying?" she asked softly. Mike looked up at her, then kissed her stomach again.

"I'm not *saying* anything."

"Oh."

"I was telling our son how much I love his mother, and that she should never not trust me, not ever again." Jono felt like she was going to pass out. Words that were the farthest from her dreams. She looked straight up at the stars, then grabbed the top of Mike's head. She dropped to her knees, inches away from his face. "I will never trust anyone one in the world the way I trust you. I love you." She crushed his face with hers, consuming his lips into her mouth. She kissed him hard, trying to give him every part of her, trying to convince his soul she was sorry.

Jono and Mike sat down on the towel, looking out over the water. About every ten seconds, Jono would look at Mike to make sure he was real, that he was still there. Mike never took his hand off of Jono's stomach. They were falling deeper in love with every second that passed. Mike stood up, and Jono got scared. *Please don't let this be over!* she screamed in her head. "How much do you love me?" Mike asked in a sincere way. Jono didn't hesitate.

"More than I could ever explain." She glanced out over the water. "More than all the water in the sea." She smiled.

"Good. I was hoping you'd say that." He reached for Jono's hand, then pulled her up and kissed her.

"Why?" Jono actually pinched herself to make sure it was real.

"I want to show you something, I think you're going to like it." He took her hand and started walking toward Dan's house. Jono was at a loss.

"What is it?" she asked. Mike, without missing a beat, told her.

"An early wedding present."

Jono fell to her knees. She put her hands down on the sand to support herself: she couldn't breathe. Mike rushed over to her.

"Are you okay?" She sat on the backs of her legs and lifted her head. "Mike," she pleaded.

Mike kneeled down on the sand right in front of her. "Jono, I know this might seem a little crazy, you know, considering the circumstances, but I love you, I want to always be with you, I want to take care of you and our son…" Jono put her finger over his lips, stopping him. She pulled his face up to hers. "Yes," she smiled sweetly. Mike smiled, then kissed her. He stood up then pulled Jono up to her feet and started walking again.

"But I don't understand… Where are you taking me?" Mike didn't answer: he and Jono walked past the side of Dan's house, trying to be quiet so they didn't wake anyone. Up the driveway, out of the gate, and down the street. "Mike?" Jono asked. Mike stopped cold. "Uh, okay, I know things have been, well, strange but you're only adding to that right now." She smiled.

Mike walked up to her and gave her a passionate kiss. Jono melted in his arms. Then he stood her up and turned her toward the house they were standing in front of. "Your wedding present," he said proudly pointing to the immediate neighbors' house. Jono laughed. She looked at the big beautiful house: it looked like there were lights on inside. Then she looked back at Mike.

"We're going to get arrested," she said calmly.

Mike took her hand again, walked through the gate straight to the massive front door. "Mike? What are you doing?" Mike smiled at Jono. Something came over her, she completely relaxed. *Now's a good time to start trusting*, she thought. She smiled back. Mike bent over and picked Jono up in his arms. "Holy crap!" Jono laughed. Mike pushed in the front door with one foot, and carried Jono over the threshold, kissing her all the way in. Jono was gone, disconnected from anything else. Mike stopped and set Jono down. Candles were burning everywhere, dozens and dozens; Hawaiian flowers were laid out all around the room, making the room smell perfect.

Jono scanned the room: it had no furniture, the house was empty. *Oh man,* she thought to herself. *What did Mike do?* Mike walked her into the middle of the room, and had her stand and wait. He ran over and pushed the all-glass walls into the house wall, opening up the entire room to the outside. "Beautiful," Jono said. "Wait." Mike disappeared out of sight. Jono was not as nervous as she would normally be, so she waited. Before she could put together one thought Mike was back with a small pillow in his hand.

'What's this?" she asked. He tossed the pillow on the floor in front of Jono. She looked at the pillow then at him. Mike smiled then got down on one knee using the pillow, Jono gasped, she held her heart with her hand while Mike took her left hand and held it close. He kissed it.

"Jono, my life has no meaning without you in it. You make me a better person. I want to be with you the rest of my life." The tears were flowing down Jono's face; she was afraid she was going to pee. "Will you marry me?" he asked as sincerely as any man ever had. Jono looked out at the ocean. She felt a breeze cutting through the house. She could smell the flowers. She wanted to remember everything; then she looked at him and smiled. "Yes." Mike stood up. He held her face in his hands, then kissed her. "I love you, Michael." Mike stepped back and picked up Jono's left hand; smoothly but powerfully he slid a ring on her finger. She looked down at her hand as Mike kissed it again. "Oh my God!" she yelled very loudly. The ring took Jono's breath away. Even with only candlelight, the ring flashed brilliant colors all around the room. She held it up close: it was huge. "Mike... oh my God." She held her hand out so she could admire the ring; she held her other hand over her mouth.

"So, you like it?" he asked, smiling. Jono hit him on the arm. "Jono's back!" he laughed.

"But Mike... this is too much. This is crazy... how is this possible?"

"You need to sit down, I have a little confession of my own." Jono's stomach suddenly wasn't doing well, her mind was racing but she refused to give in to her thoughts; besides Troy already admitted he was the one. *So what's going on?* she questioned herself. Jono took a breath and sat down on the pillow. Mike ran into the kitchen and got them both some water then came and sat on the floor in front of Jono.

"Mike, before you start, I have to ask you something."

"Sure."

"How did you know? I mean how did you know I'd be here, looking for you?" she asked. Mike smiled.

"That was a hell of a right hook!" he chuckled.

"You saw? You knew?" Jono was about to attack, but Mike held her back. "Right, sorry. Go ahead. I'm anxious to hear this story." Jono smiled, and Mike nodded.

"So..." Mike went on to explain to Jono everything that she didn't know about him and his past. Jono sat quietly trying to listen, but was more focused on Mike's face, fantasizing about their life together. Then Mike got to a part of the story that snapped her out of her little daydream.

"I'm sorry, I think I missed that. Can you repeat that last part again," she asked. She heard Mike speak about his former life as a fireman, his first wife and his young daughter, but then he explained what happened after their deaths.

"Well, I already told you the owner of the boat was from Saudi Arabia. He left the country before any charges could be filed."

"Yes, I remember."

"What I didn't tell you, or anyone till just recently, was this guy, the owner of the boat, is a young prince from one of the richest families in Saudi Arabia. At the time, I couldn't care less. I didn't even want to press charges, I just didn't care. But around a month later, a man wearing a suit approached me on the beach. He asked me to come with him. It seemed important, so I did. I was all nasty and dirty, but he took me into his big fancy office in a downtown bank and asked me to sit down."

"Wow, that's a little crazy."

"I know. I was so out of it, he could have been anybody taking me anywhere. So, he talked to me for a few minutes. To this day I can't remember what he said. Then he set down two sheets of paper in front of me. He asked me to sign them, which I did, then he stood up, thanked me and escorted me back out of the bank."

"What the heck? What did you sign?" Jono was more than curious.

"It turns out I signed an affidavit saying that I would never file charges or a lawsuit against this young prince and I would never pursue him or his family in any way."

"Wow. But I guess that makes sense. And why not take advantage while you were, you know, down. And the second piece of paper? What was that for?"

"Well, the prince felt so bad about what he did, especially after seeing the news accounts of the incident, that he sent me what he thought was appropriate compensation for the death of my wife and daughter. When I signed, I was agreeing to the amount."

"Really? That's just sad, isn't it? I'm so sorry, that had to be terrible. What a crazy story, I'm glad you told me, though."

"It's important that you know and understand."

"Yes, of course, so that's how you were able to buy this amazing ring? Which I love. It's the most beautiful ring I've ever seen." She leaned over and kissed him.

"It is..."

"What?"

"Well, I didn't buy just the ring... I also bought this house." He smiled. Jono stayed perfectly still, her mouth hanging open, staring at Mike. Mike smiled. "I hope you like the house, I hear it's a good neighborhood." He chuckled.

"Mike... you're teasing me, right? You didn't really buy this house, did you?" She had an indescribable look on her face. Mike smiled again. "You did! So, you're telling me... this is *our* house?" Mike nodded. Jono tackled him right there on the floor. They made love like it was the first time, only occasionally coming up for water. They fell asleep on the floor naked in the middle of their new home. The sun woke up Mike a few hours later. He woke up Jono who was stiff and sore, but smiling.

"Holy smoke!" she yelped.

"What is it?" Mike asked. Jono smiled.

"Hold on." She grabbed her phone and called Maxwell. "Well hello?"

"Are you up yet?"

"Of course, honey, we need to leave in like twenty minutes. Where are you?"

"Maxwell, gather everyone in the living room, including Kaleen and Kale. I'll be right there!" Then she abruptly hung up. "Well, that was just rude." Maxwell smiled. "I love it when she's like that!" Jono threw on her bathing suit and wrapped her towel as tightly as she could around her. She explained to Mike what she wanted to do; Mike was already ahead of her. Five minutes later she was ringing the front door at Dan's house. Kaleen opened the door, and Jono leaped into her arms. Kaleen hugged her hard: she could feel the energy in Jono's body. Kaleen stepped back and smiled: she knew. "Jono! What's going on? We've got to get going? You need to hurry up and change," Maxwell barked at her.

Jono stepped into the middle of the room. She turned slowly and looked at everyone. "I need a favor," she told them. Most nodded; others looked on curiously. "I know I've already asked too much of you, but I promise this favor is different." She paused. "I need you to extend your trips, you can't leave, not now," she said gleefully. They looked at her like maybe she was drunk or something; they all just stared. "Jono, what are you talking about? Why do you want us to stay and why do you need help?" Maxwell spoke for the group. Jono was about to burst, but she let it out slowly.

"I need your help… because… I'm getting married!" she yelled loudly, spinning around flashing her ring. Before anyone could say a word or react in any way Mike walked through the front door. Still only wearing a bathing suit, he walked to the tiled edge of the landing. He smiled. "Hi, guys."

"Holy shit!" Maxwell jumped to his feet. "It's Mike!" He quickly walked over to him, shook his hand and gave him a hug.

"We've combed this island for days looking for you, we were just about to go home."

Mike smiled. "Yes, Jono told me the whole story. I'm sorry about that."

"No, that's okay, I'm just glad you're here, and you're okay. You're definitely okay." Maxwell gave him the once-over and smiled.

Jono came up behind Maxwell and hugged him. Maxwell pulled her in front of him.

"This is really happening? I can't believe it. Let me see this trinket." He reached out for Jono's hand. "Oh my, *this* is a thing of beauty." Jono was on a cloud. "You guys, come over here and check out Jono's ring!" Maxwell yelled to the rest of the group. They all took turns looking at the ring, congratulating Mike and Jono and giving out hugs.

"This is so amazing!" Holly shouted out. "I can't believe you found Mike… and now you're getting married! It's amazing, Jono!" Then she paused. "I still don't understand why you want us to stay?" she asked. "Are you going to have a party or something?"

Jono stepped next to Mike and put her arm around his waist; she looked at him. He smiled. "With your help we'd like to get married two weeks from today," Mike announced. "Right here on the beach." Everyone started clapping and cheering. Maxwell was flush with happiness. He stepped back and watched Jono and Mike: they were so happy. "Thank God!" he thought. "She is finally getting what she deserves!" Kaleen came to Jono: she couldn't have had a bigger smile.

"No Keia La, No Keia Po, A Mau Loa" (From this day, from this night, for evermore), she said to Jono, then hugged her. Jono looked over to Mike, and he smiled. "It's a good thing." Kaleen moved to Mike: she was beaming like a proud mother. "Mahalo E Ke Akua No Keia La" (Thanks be to God for this day). Mike leaned over and hugged her. "Mahalo," he said to her.

Kaleen was the rarest of people. She loved with an open hand and heart. She lived to give, even though she and Kale had never had a lot of money, they always found other ways. Kaleen was sixty-five, Kale sixty-eight. They met in high school on one of the other islands, then they moved to Oahu after Kale joined the post-war effort. It was the perfect setting for Kaleen: she was able to give, love and support twenty-four hours a day. They'd been married for what Kale refers to as *forty-seven magical years*. Sadly, due to smallpox when Kaleen was a child, she became sterile, taking away any chance of having children of their own. They fostered many children over the years, which they enjoyed greatly. But after getting hired by Dan five years ago, they had to give it up. "I've always had one child," Kaleen would joke about Kale.

"Champagne!" Maxwell yelled out. Everyone cheered. Kaleen and Holly were on it. After everyone received their glass of bubbly, Maxwell cleared his throat to get everyone's attention. He held his glass high in the air, and everyone followed his gesture.

"To Mike and Jono…" He had to stop for a second to get his composure back. "Can you believe I'm doing this?" he lovingly smiled. Everyone laughed. "Aren't we all supposed to be on a plane right about now? This is truly amazing, and I'm so happy to be a part of it… So…" He cleared his throat again. "To Mike and Jono. May you always have love, peace and respect, oh and trust!" he chuckled. "To Mike and Jono!" he raised his glass higher. "To Mike and Jono!" everyone repeated. Jono took the tiniest sip of her champagne; she didn't want to miss out on the toast. "So I guess we have a wedding to plan!" Maxwell yelled excitedly. Everyone cheered. Jono held her tummy and looked at Mike. "I deserve you." "I know," he smiled.

ABOUT THE AUTHOR

Dutch Jones is an Author, Blogger & Entrepreneur. He lives to write, loves to blog, and is a zealot for business. Dutch represents the true meaning of what it is to be a Storyteller. "I feel it's my position in life to entertain you through my writings." Other recent releases include Long Trip Home and E.A.P. The Untold Story.

Made in the USA
San Bernardino, CA
01 March 2015